Blocke

Jeremy Moorhouse

Acknowledgements & Dedication

This one's for you Helen. The original, brilliant idea for the theme came from you. Thank you so much. I hope you laugh as much when you read it as I did while I wrote it.

Sam finished rinsing out the teapot and propped it on the drainer. "Rock down to electric avenue…" he sang along with Eddie.

The front door thumped loudly.

He could hear Miranda huffing and tutting as she tugged her coat off.

Nigel was on his paws and through to the inner porch door with his usual enthusiasm. As a spaniel, he considered it his duty to make sure that anyone who entered was properly checked to see what manner of food they were bringing into his house.

"Hello gorgeous boy." Miranda greeted her happily waggling familiar. She paused in the hall for the essential greetings and then stomped through to the kitchen where she dumped her bag and a carrier full of groceries onto the kitchen worktop.

"Everything okay?" Sam asked, knowing full well from the thumping and huffing that it clearly wasn't.

"That bloody taxi driver looks at me like I'm a sodding racehorse!" came the reply.

Sam knew from experience that a full account was about to follow and responded diplomatically with a simple "Oh."

He skilfully plucked the bottle of Soave from the carrier

and asked, "Would now be a good time?"

Miranda made a fuss of Nigel until a brimming glass was presented. She swiftly swallowed half the contents and held it out for a refill. She was still frowning.

"He actually told me that he was going to take me for a coffee, and that he was paying!" Her tone was bewildered exasperation.

"Oh dear" Sam responded, "Shall I tell him you don't like coffee?"

"No. Thank you. I don't need you to tell him anything. In fact don't! Don't say a word. I'm perfectly capable of dealing with this myself."

When Miranda began speaking in abrupt sentences, Sam knew that for the moment, his role was to listen. "Do you want to tell me from the beginning?"

Sam already knew that Miranda had taken a dislike to walking past the taxi rank on her way in and out of town. Miranda was sociable by nature, and so a casual 'Good morning' had grown into short conversations and now, two of the taxi drivers had developed the delusion that Miranda was flirting with them.

There had been several discussions about this already. Miranda had her own unique style; she dressed smartly and was generally cheerful and bright. It attracted attention, attention Miranda really didn't want or appreciate. As far as Miranda was concerned, she wore what she liked and felt comfortable in, not some outfit to turn her into something akin to a show-pony.

It had become a recurring theme. When she was working away, she could walk through any city, and most people didn't give her a second glance. She blended in with the general crowd.

Here, at home in their little market town, heads turned, and people gawped, especially when Sam and Miranda walked down the street together.

Sam had lived in Sedgewood all his life, and everyone knew him. Sam Boycott, the market garden man. Sam grew vegetables, sold plants and hanging baskets, and was *the* expert locally when it came to reclaiming any garden which had reverted to wilderness.

In the warmer months, he would usually be dressed in sun faded shorts, bramble torn tee-shirts and scuffed dusty work boots.

Miranda was a head taller than Sam, even taller with her hat on, and whatever she wore, she always looked elegant. While other women complimented her , men snuck glances. Miranda didn't appreciate it.

"I think I'm just going to walk around Parliament Avenue way from now on." Miranda concluded.

"But you shouldn't have to" Sam answered "Surely you can just tell him you're not interested? He knows we're married anyway, what's wrong with him?"

"He's like a lot of people darling. He doesn't respect boundaries." Miranda replied with a familiar finality. Miranda knew a lot about boundaries. She wrote for a bestselling magazine covering all sorts of relationship dynamics.

"I know I could tell him, but right now, I really don't want to have to. I'll walk the long way."

Sam knew that Miranda would often ponder a situation for days or even weeks before she delivered her response. When she did, it would be thoughtful, measured and sometimes devastating. Sam knew better than to interfere with Miranda's processes. It was one of the main reasons they'd stayed together through all their trials.

The kitchen filled with the aroma of onions and cumin as he scraped the chopping board into the frying pan.
The conversation was interrupted by the doorbell.
"I'll get it." Miranda volunteered. Sam continued assembling the chilli he'd been working on.
Nigel beat her to the front door and then growled.
Miranda knew instantly what that meant and turned back into the kitchen having seen a familiar silhouette through the glass in the doors.
"I'm not going to answer that." She informed Sam then added "Nigel growled"
"Oh bless him" Sam knew immediately what that was about too. "Roger by any chance?"
"How did you know?" Miranda laughed. "He's a neighbourhood watch all by himself that man. I'm definitely not in the mood for him this evening. That smells good."

Later that evening as Sam readied himself for bed, Miranda called something to him.

"I can't hear you" he called back down the stairs, "I'm cleaning my teeth. Give me a minute?"

"Hmmph werfff shleepp cromff" he heard coming back up the stairs in response. He finished brushing and rinsing and plodded back down the stairs.

"What did you say?"

"I said that bloody creep has only found my Farcebook profile and sent me a flipping friends request."

"Who? Keith? Why don't you add him then?" Sam answered with a mischievous twinkle in his eye, "We could wind him up like a spinning top?"

Miranda laughed. Sam was a constant source of entertainment, even if some of his ideas were a little ill-advised.

"No!" she answered firmly, "I'll just block him. Honestly, I wish I could just have a magic button where I could block him in real life, not just social media. That would be my super-power if I had one!"

Unseen by either of them, Miranda's Spirit guide sat quietly on the end of the sofa. She smiled broadly. She'd been waiting patiently for months for Miranda to ask for something. In fact, Freya had been feeling quite redundant just recently as she'd watched Miranda struggling, but stubbornly refusing to ask anyone, let alone her Spirit guide, for help.

'Ask and it is given' said some of the thousands of offerings on manifesting and Cosmic ordering.

Freya knew that in principle, the idea was good, if a little vague about how to actually affect the universe in a way that was truly desired.

She'd waited a long time for Miranda to ask for something though, and Freyas job was to grant wishes…as long as they served a genuine purpose of course. And this particular wish thoroughly appealed to Freya's sense of naughtiness.

If Miranda and Sam had been able to hear it, they would have heard a noise quite similar to the opening of a rosebud. As the petals unfurled, tiny droplets of cosmic magic emerged from the infinite sea of possibilities. Freya smiled to herself. That was a job well done. Now it was up to Miranda how she used her new superpower, and how she lived with the consequences.

The magic began working subtly. Miranda went to bed with the idea of a super-power lodged firmly in her imagination. At half past one, she gave up trying to sleep. Sam was snoring anyway. Soon he would undoubtedly come out with one of his bewildering sleep announcements. "Not that way round! It's the purple ones." Had been his most recent offering. Heaven only knew what his dreamscape looked like. Miranda took herself off into the spare room. Nigel was quick to join her.

They often ended up like this. Nigel would contentedly sprawl out beside her while Miranda mentally assembled her compositions for the magazine. By the time the dawn chorus began, Miranda would have a fully formed article in her head and would dictate it into her phone ready to be finished properly just a few hours later.

There were some occasions when Sam was nocturnal too. Always protective of his plants, he was especially vigilant when the weather invoked greater snail mobility. Neighbourhood watch Roger had called the police on several occasions because Sam had had the audacity to patrol his own garden with a torch looking for the slimy villains. Admittedly it was 3am, but surely that was Sam's business?

As for Roger, well, the man didn't appear to sleep. He was like some sort of vampire, only Roger fed on knowing everyone else's private business.

Miranda turned her attention back to the big red hexagonal button she kept visualising.

In her mind's eye, she could see it plainly. The image was uncannily clear, and the word BLOCKED stood out in 3D relief in sharp white letters.

As she examined it in greater detail, she noticed something which looked like the top of a funnel protruding from the top edge. The flute disappeared into the heart of the button.

How would this work exactly? She gave the matter some consideration. If she really could block people, she didn't just want them to vanish from her social media, she'd rather like it if they buggered off altogether.

But they mustn't get hurt of course.

Miranda had invested a huge body of time investigating

near death experiences and reports of the afterlife. She'd come to the conclusion that the notion of Karma was simply bypassing. No need for anyone to take responsibility because the magic super invisible sky daddy will punish all the infringements right?
Well, no actually, Miranda had concluded.

She was also pretty certain that Hell was just a device the Christians had employed to terrify their recruitment base. If Hell had been real, then most of the priesthood and sisterhood were surely going there? It just didn't ring true. Why hadn't other people made the link, such as all the Bishops and Cardinals who definitely knew it was codswallop?
How else could they behave the way they did?

And who exactly sat in Judgement? In the Egyptian version, Thoth, Osiris, and Anubis all got together apparently, but who had the final word?
Miranda wasn't convinced by any of the conventional theories, but she couldn't quite shake off the idea that there was some sort of inevitable accountability. Consequently, throughout her adult life, no matter what the circumstance, she had done her best to live by the maxim, 'Be who you are , just don't be a git.'
It worked for her.

So where would anyone she blocked go then?
She took the ultimate spiritual cop-out and announced, "I'm leaving where they end up to my Guardian Angel to sort out!"

Unseen in the dim moonlight, Nigel looked at her and rolled his eyes.

It was almost 2.45 now. Some people claimed that midnight was the witching hour. The slightly better informed knew that really, it was 3am.
So who would she block? Miranda began to compile a list. Well those two from the taxi rank would be going. That patronising twerp from the whole food shop needed to disappear too. Michael, her brother, he could go, and his boring wife, Doreen. Oh boy, at the last family wedding, Miranda had been stuck on a table with Doreen for almost three hours. Trying to make conversation with the woman was like pulling hens teeth. She didn't have a sense of humour either. The minutes had stretched into hours. Miranda had graduated almost instantly from table wine to Tequila just to get through the most excruciating toasts and speeches, interspersed by Doreen's completely irrelevant banal offerings about what was going on at the sailing club.

Sleep was coming now, and Miranda decided to go for one last wee. Nigel thought he'd try his luck and as Miranda came out of the bathroom, on the dim moonlit landing, gave her his very best 'I'm hungry' face.
"Oh come on then" she responded. Nigel would get two breakfasts today. It didn't matter though, as a Springer, he soon burned off any excess calories simply by being his usual cheerful self.
They made their way quietly down to the kitchen.
Nigel was usually highly attentive when the cupboard containing his biscuits was opened, but tonight, he went

straight to the back door.

"Oh well, go on then, as we're up"

Miranda turned the key and pulled the door open.

Nigel growled. Nigel only ever growled at one person.

Miranda could see the shadowy but unmistakable figure attempting to scurry away from the back door.

"Roger! What the fuck are you doing in my garden again?"

Nigel growled some more.

"Oh Hi Miranda. Nothing to worry about. I was just doing the rounds." He waved his hands in a placatory gesture.

"I'll say that again Roger. What the fuck are you doing in my garden?"

Roger was well known for his unwelcome prowling around the Close with a torch in the dead of night.

To date, since Miranda and Sam had lived in their house, the only property on the whole estate to have ever been burgled had been Rogers. As it happened, while he was out sneaking around everyone else's.

He claimed he was neighbourhood watching. Miranda, like most of her neighbours, suspected he was a peeping tom. She couldn't stand the man.

"Get out of my garden IMMEDIATELY and don't ever set foot in it again!" Then she clicked her fingers at Nigel "You can bite him if you like?"

Roger didn't wait and took off up the path at the side of the house as fast as he could travel. In the darkness he found the stone badger ornament Sam's mum had given them. There was a yelp and Roger went down with a wet

gravelly thud before scrambling to his feet and taking off
again.

Nigel, his work done, padded happily back into the kitchen.
Some of Mirandas anger shifted to amusement, that must
have hurt.

Nigel just looked puzzled. Bite someone? Nigel didn't bite
people.

Miranda locked the door and went and checked the front
door before clambering back up the stairs and into bed.

Roger. That was who could go. In her mind's eye, she
imagined Roger standing in front of her, dressed in his
favourite green anorak, torch in one hand, mouth
gormlessly hanging open, as usual.

She reached out and pressed the button. The last thing she
saw before sleep took her in it's comforting embrace, was
an image of Roger becoming smaller and smaller, and then
disappearing into the funnel at the top of the button.

The small carriage clock in her office softly chimed three
times.

There was also another very different sound. It was almost
identical to the sound the flush used to make on her
grandmothers ancient cast iron toilet cistern, but much,
much quieter.

Roger hadn't made it very far from Miranda and Sam's house. Miranda had been right; he'd gone down with a bang. It was only the thought of being bitten that had raised him to his feet again so quickly. Thank goodness she hadn't opened the door a few minutes earlier. He'd been right inside the greenhouse then. If he'd realised that anyone was awake at that hour, he'd have come later. Roger really did like to know what was going on.

He checked behind him once more just to make sure that bloody dog wasn't following him, and then limped the last few meters into Mrs Buchanan's garden where he promptly sagged on the bench.

Mrs Buchanan had passed away about a month ago although Roger knew from his patrols that virtually all of her things were still inside the bungalow. Her sons had emptied the fridge and had been to collect the post but otherwise, the home was as she'd left it. Roger knew this for certain as he'd discovered the spare key hidden outside several years previously. He still had a copy on his 'special' bunch.

His trouser leg was torn and covered in blood. What was he going to tell Norma?

He felt the most peculiar sensation come over him. He must have banged his head harder than he'd realised. He felt dizzy. Everything seemed to be spinning. His body felt as if it was shrinking, and what on earth was that noise? It sounded just like a toilet flushing. The world spun and then winked momentarily out of existence. Roger lost consciousness altogether at that point.

There was a small plop, and Rogers slumped body rematerialized in an almost identical copy of the universe he'd just come from. Identical in every way that was except that in this universe, Roger was the only human being present.

For just a short while anyway.

Miranda woke to the sound of Sam making his customary racket in the bathroom. For a man who could move so deftly around the house, he crashed around the bathroom in a way that resembled a rhino on a trampoline. More than once, Miranda had asked him whether everything was okay? These days she understood he was just habitually clumsy in the mornings, hence the accompanying bangs and thuds.

Nigel peered at her hopefully from the half-closed bedroom door. She fumbled for her phone. "Urrgg! Oh god Nigel, 5.50am." Sam always left early on a Friday. By 8am he'd have unloaded his van and be all set up in the marketplace. If Miranda were working from home, she'd generally walk into town at around nine-o-clock and take him a hot bacon roll and a mug of the best tea in town from Sedgewood's little café on the market square. Sometimes they'd spend a few hours working the stall together.

Miranda loved meeting the shoppers. She also took the opportunity to study them and lead their conversations gently in a manner which helped give her insight into her current magazine-article topic.
The articles were always written months ahead of publication. There was rarely any recognition between the people she chatted to and the content of her pieces. Miranda was also particularly adept at signposting people to help, without them realising that was what had happened. Sam viewed his customers as a friendly bunch who wanted vegetables and plants. Miranda viewed them as a mainly

troubled group with some often, quite spectacularly toxic relationship dynamics.

She was working on a four-page spread about co-dependency at the moment. Today would be a great day to get some research done.

She looked at Nigel again and said softly "Alright then gorgeous, you can come too."

The spaniel had no idea what she was talking about, but he smiled at her anyway.

Miranda knew that sometimes, people would stop to say hello to Nigel, whereas they might have carried on walking past her and Sam if they'd been dogless. Without a doubt, a springer spaniel was a great way to meet people. And Nigel was especially beautiful after all.

There was a bang as Sam burst out of the bathroom and the door clattered on the wall. Miranda shuffled through for her turn.

By the time Miranda got downstairs, Sam had almost finished his coffee. Some mornings Nigel went with him, and some days the happy spaniel stayed at home with his mum. Two big brown eyes kept looking from one to the other trying to work out what today would bring, and whether he might be able to help with that last bit of toast Sam obviously didn't want. Nigel could smell the marmite.

"I'm guessing you didn't hear our visitor last night then?" Miranda lifted the kettle to refill it.

"Erm no?" Between mouthfuls of coffee and toast. "Has that fox been back then?"

Miranda turned and explained. "No love, not a fox, a

Roger!" She proceeded to explain what had happened.
Sam was angry. "Well I hope he hurt himself properly. I'll
bloody hurt him if he comes round here again. What the
hell's he up to? I really do think it's time we put in a formal
complaint now. You're the one who knows all about
boundaries after all."

"Yes you're right love. I've had enough too. He makes my
skin crawl. There's something seriously wrong with that
man. I feel so sorry for his sister. She's got no chance of
having a life while he's around. I bet he's horrible behind
closed doors
I'll call the station and make it formal just as soon as you're
away." Then she added in a more relaxed tone "Would you
like some company today?"
Sam brightened up a notch. "I would. That'd be great."
"I'll bring our boy with me then; it'll save you doing
morning collections."
Sam loved his dog as much as he loved his wife. What he
really didn't like though, was having to pick up Nigel's
monumental offerings just after breakfast every morning.
Thank the gods he didn't have to do that for Miranda.
It was 6.45 now, Sam needed to get moving.
"I love you." He answered, and then he was gone.

Miranda made a pot of tea and picked up her phone to
check her messages. Damn! She'd forgotten about the
creepy friend request from taxi-Keith.
"You're blocked chum!" she said pushing the confirm
button. In her mind's eye, she saw the big hexagonal button
again. Her phone seemed to make a soft plopping noise.

On the taxi rank just a few hundred yards away, a passenger began climbing into the second car in the queue. "I'd like to go to the station please" came the standard enquiry. "Oh sorry mate, you'll need to jump in the one in front. We always work that way."

"Ah, well I was going to, but there doesn't appear to be a driver."

"Oh. Really? I wonder where Keith went? I'm sure he was there a minute ago."

Norma Parkinson had woken to an unusually quiet house. By now, Roger would usually be in the room he called the operations centre, with four different screens playing four different versions of the news.

Roger had a fold up bed in the room, although he never seemed to use it. Sleep was something other people did, not Roger Parkinson. Roger fed on other peoples energy.

Norma called softly at the door. It stank of sweat and mildew. "Roger, are you in there?" She wasn't allowed to go in normally. Roger claimed the room as his personal domain, even though their parents had left the house entirely to Norma. After their passing, she'd been completely powerless when he'd moved his belongings back into the house from his grotty little caravan.

Roger had dominated his sister and she'd financially supported him ever since he'd been sacked from his job. Roger had said that Sedgewood leisure centre had been making cutbacks. Normas best friend Suzie, who'd had a cleaning job there at the time, had told a different story. Roger had liked to tell the junior members of staff that he worked for MI5 and that consequently, his job was to keep an eye on certain people.

The police had been involved. Roger had been charged with multiple counts of stalking and invasions of privacy.

He definitely wasn't in there; Norma poked her head around the door frame for the first time in over three years. The mess would have shocked the most hardened pathologist, but Norma smiled anyway. Roger wasn't there!

A dozen thoughts rushed through Norma's head all at

once. Perhaps her brother had been captured by someone he'd been spying on? Perhaps he'd been really badly beaten up? Or really well beaten up of course, depending on your perspective? She grinned a little more broadly. Perhaps he'd had an accident? If so, she hoped it was something serious. He was such a creature , creature being the appropriate word, of habit, he was always home by 6am. It was almost 7.45 now. Norma grinned even more hopefully. What if he'd been arrested? He'd had so many cautions in the past, there was no way he was going to escape prison this time. Whatever it was, his energy was fading. Norma had been well accomplished psychically before her brother had come to haunt the house. There was no doubt in her mind now though, he was genuinely gone.

Norma practically skipped through to the kitchen where she announced "Alexa. Play Oh Happy Day by the Edwin Hawkins Singers."

In a universe less than an atoms width from this one, Roger Parkinson slowly regained consciousness. He was lying on a cold, wet lawn. His knee stung like fire and his head was throbbing. His stomach felt as if he'd just done half a dozen consecutive turns on the waltzers.

"Chirp-chirp-chirp-chirp-chirp-chirp" The bright orange beak of an agitated blackbird came into focus at first and Miranda Boycotts face seemed to float in front of him momentarily, and then, an image of her bloody dog.

Roger had to get home, and quickly at that. If that Boycott woman reported him, he would need to have his journal ready, and an alibi.

What time was it anyway?

Roger tugged at his sleeve to reveal his military style tactical watch. "Oh my god" he gasped; it was 7.45. There would be people everywhere. Friday was market day. How many people might have seen him lying on Mrs Buchanan's lawn? And yet, apart from the birdsong and the rustle of the wind in the sycamores, it was strangely quiet. The air smelt remarkably clean too.

Roger clambered to his feet. Home was just under half a mile away. Roger knew exactly which way to go to avoid being seen by too many people except, there wasn't anyone. Certainly, there were cars parked on driveways, but on the road, not a single vehicle, nor could he hear any. Where were all the ruddy kids? They should have been out crawling the streets on their way to school by now, but there wasn't a single voice, or footstep or football clanging into a garage door. There weren't any buses either, or dog

walkers, or taxis.
Something was very wrong here.

Miranda did her best to support her little local corner shop. She would pop in at least three or four times a week, even though she could have bought the same things on her way through town.

In the face of overwhelming corporatisation, she understood clearly just how important it was to keep small businesses alive. Sam supplied them with vegetables too, so it was good politics to pop in from time to time.

What she found off-putting was that Joy, the owner, really did enjoy a good gossip. Not much went on in Sedgewood which escaped thorough public dissection in amongst the baked beans and envelopes.

Joy was a better broadcaster than Radio Mellow, the local radio station.

Joy also had a habit of getting things wrong. On the plus side as a journalist, Miranda found some of Joy's interpretations of words hilarious.

Miranda often came away pondering how ironically Joy's parents had named her. She was one of the dourest people Miranda had to deal with.

Miranda tried hard to restrict her interactions to the minimum and neither comment nor volunteer anything which would most certainly be repeated within five minutes of her stepping outside again.

She braced herself as she tied Nigel up to the dog rail.

Sure enough, Joy was in full flow "…and I didn't know where to look. Talk about a bikini line, it was more like an essay…, Oh Hi Miranda, you okay love? How's your Sam doing? I saw his new hanging baskets on the market. Them Derangiums look bootiful."

Miranda wondered whether she'd taken a deep enough breath before entering. Joy certainly knew how to consume all the oxygen in the room.

Joy was on a roll. "Have you heard about the taxi this morning?"

As the incident had only occurred just two hours ago, this was unlikely, and Joy knew when she had a precious nugget. If she kept her latest subject talking, in this case Miranda, she might learn one or two other useful gems. What some people called gossip; Joy knew was currency. She didn't wait for an answer and with all the enthusiasm she usually enjoyed for someone else's misfortune, began to explain. "You know Keith the taxi? Lovely man! He's in and out of here all the time you know? Well, he just vanished this morning apparently, like into thin air."

Miranda had been about to select a packet of biscuits but now, Joy had her full attention. She turned to face her slowly. Joy had her on the hook, she carried on hurriedly before Miranda could interrupt the narrative.

"One minute he was in his car at the front of the rank, the next he was gone, like magic, and no one saw him go, and he left the engine running and everyfink. Aren't you and him friends?"

Miranda bristled visibly. Joy knew she was onto something now.

"And who exactly told you we were friends?" Miranda managed between clenched teeth. She'd been happy enough saying good morning to him, or even "It's a lovely day." But friends? In whose mind had they been friends? Certainly not hers.

"Oh he used to say you stopped and chatted with him

every time you saw him. I thought from what he said that you two were quite close?" Came the reply from behind the counter. Obviously either Keith had been expanding his delusion or Joy had been feasting on other snippets of small-town gossip. Probably a little of both Miranda decided.

"No, we're not friends, and as far as I know, never have been. I'll take these thank you." Miranda presented a packet of ginger nuts with a finality that even Joy was able to recognise.

Just as she was about to step back outside, she turned back to Joy and said, "And what time did he disappear exactly?"

"Barry Tomkins was in the line behind him, and he said it was about seven o clock. Why?"

"Oh nothing really. Just wondered."

Joy, Miranda decided, should definitely have worked for the police. As irritating as she was, she had a nose for information like a truffle pig.

Miranda exited and untied Nigel. She'd planned to head into town, but now she decided to walk along the river instead.

Two hours ago? She checked her watch; it was twelve minutes past nine. Keith couldn't have really vanished? He must have just nipped off somewhere. Surely the timing was just coincidence? Yes, that was it, she was just imagining things. Nothing to do with her. He'd probably just gone to sleaze around another of his chosen targets. There were probably dozens of women he'd tried to coerce into 'coffee.' No doubt Keith would turn up again and there would be a perfectly logical explanation why he'd left his engine running.

On Blocked world, in Keiths head, apart from momentarily experiencing a strange shrinking sensation, accompanied with a distant sound like a toilet flushing, there was no immediate discernible change.

There he was, sitting in his cab at the front of the rank waiting for the next fare. Keith knew that once the first ride was in, he'd be busy ferrying continuous fares around Sedgewood until around 11am. Then there would be the inevitable lull where he could go and use the toilet and grab another cup of coffee.

He decided to check his social media to see if any of the eight or nine friends requests he'd sent out yesterday had been answered. That was odd, his phone was charged, but there was no signal and the opening screen was blank. It must be faulty he told himself. Flippin technology.

He lifted his head to gaze at the street. What he saw filled him with the same feeling of discomfort as the day he'd watched the total solar eclipse. It wasn't butterflies in the pit of his stomach; it was camels.

It was just after 7am and the streets of Sedgemoor ought to be full of people beginning their day. Just a second earlier, they had been.

Where on earth had everyone gone? He was alone on the rank too. There were no cars on the road and the three other cabs which had been patiently waiting behind him had all vanished. There weren't any pedestrians or cyclists either.

He reached for his radio. "Control? Control? Can you hear me?"

No-one answered.

Keith decided he'd drive up to the Forty, it was usually quite busy up there at this time of day.

The town of Sedgemoor was set in a beautiful rural landscape of rolling hills and chalk downland. Two villages had expanded over centuries until they'd touched boundaries and blended into one. There were still thatched cottages and timber framed houses here. All around the little railway station was a collection of art deco style three- and four-bedroom houses from the 1930's with their distinctive rounded steel windows. On the eastern side was a collection of brick-built cottages which surrounded the old village green. Opposite was a small cluster of shops and the village post office. The Forty was named after the forty paces young lads would have to stride from the firing position to the target when they took part in their obligatory longbow practice, it dated back to the thirteenth century.

The river, not much greater than a stream really, flowed through the very heart of all this. It was an image of rural England most people only ever dreamed of, and it buzzed very gently with life, normally.

Joy's Corner shop was here. Sam Boycott the gardener lived close by with that gorgeous wife of his too. There were swings and a duckpond, and the main bus stop where all the kids from that side of town would clamber abord the smelly diesel fume puffing buses in order to travel to the secondary school.

When Keith arrived, having passed not a single other moving vehicle or pedestrian, the only thing in motion around the Forty were a few small birds and a cluster of ducks. Keith felt sick. He tried his cab radio again. Nothing. It didn't even hiss with static. He'd go and see whether Linda was okay back in the flat they used as the control room shortly. First though, he'd go and ask Joy what was going on. If anyone knew anything at all, it would be Joy.

Everything about the shop looked normal when Keith walked in. "Hello" he called, hopefully. The silence that answered was the same as his attempt on the radio. There was milk in the fridge and bread on the shelves Keith noticed, but when he got to the newspaper stand, although it was filled with pages of folded paper all cut to the right sizes, the front pages were completely blank. "Hello, Joy? Are you here love?" he called again. He could hear the fear creeping into his own voice. Still no answer. He plucked a newspaper from the rack and opened it randomly. All the pages were blank. He let it drop to the floor.

Keith looked behind the counter and then stuck his head around the end by the meat slicer to peep into the storeroom. Joy wasn't there either. The door of the little lavatory was open, aside from a mop and bucket, that was unoccupied too. For the briefest of moments, Keith paused to ponder the wisdom of keeping cleaning equipment in the same place people performed their ablutions, but his overriding need was to actually find someone, anyone. He shoved the toilet door shut before turning away.

"JOY!" he called loudly one more time, and then "ANYONE? IS THERE ANYBODY THERE?"

As if he were a medium being answered by spirit, the mop fell over. Keith almost leapt out of his skin.

He had one last quick glance around the shop and was just about to leave when something new occurred to him. He snatched a magazine from the top of the rack. Underneath the plastic wrapper, the pages were as blank as the newspaper had been.

It was mid-afternoon when Miranda decided to take Nigel back home. The happy springer had had a lovely day. He'd been offered a selection of pasties, sausage rolls, cheese sandwiches and fish and chips from a whole series of admirers.

Sam was happy, he'd completely sold out of hanging baskets and tubs, and his first earlies, Charlottes, had virtually sailed off the market bench.

Sam's spuds were both well-known and highly praised in Sedgewood. Sam took great pride in them; he called them his love spuds.

Any surplus vegetables he had at the end of the day would go to their friend Tim at The Wizards Staff.

A note would be made, and Sam and Tim, friends since school days, had their own system of exchange. Tim would use the vegetables in the pub kitchen, and Sam and Miranda rarely paid for a drink or a meal there.

It was their wedding anniversary next weekend. They'd be able to celebrate in the same place they'd had their reception, and it had only cost Sam some beans. He chuckled to himself at that one.

Miranda had been chatting away all morning. The missing taxi driver hadn't been mentioned by anyone else. He'd either turned up again, or the jungle telegraph was slower than usual today. Her conscience alleviated, she kept telling herself what a silly thought it was that she could have genuinely caused a person, even a sleaze like Keith, to disappear.

On a deeply intuitive level however, Miranda knew that something out of the ordinary had occurred. She just didn't know quite what that looked like.

She decided to focus on her next article. Co-dependency and dysfunctional family dynamics. There was no shortage of raw material right here in Sedgemoor. Miranda thought back to her own childhood, and her experiences working in offices in cities around the country. At one time, Miranda had been a people pleaser, cooperative, co-dependant, manipulable and self-sabotaging. In her mid-thirties though, a string of deeply unpleasant incidents had led Miranda into the dark work of personal exploration. It had been a painful process, but an empowering one. These days Miranda was assertive, self-assured, and focussed on her own goals.

Miranda understood boundaries, and woe betide anyone who violated hers.

"Time to go home and get some writing done then" She affirmed and kissed Sam briefly before setting off back to their nest.

Unseen by the living humans but looking on from their place in the spirit world, Freya, and a trio of Mirandas other spirit guides cheered her on. Things were getting interesting now. From their perspective, they could see both the original Sedgewood and the place they were all now calling Blocked-World.

"What do you expect she'll do next?" asked Brown Cloud, Mirandas native American guide.

"I expect she'll sort out at least a couple more before the weekend's done." suggested Artimis as she mock drew her bow and loosed an invisible arrow.

"Do you think we need to have a chat with some of the blocked ones guides?" Asked Nostradamus.

"Everything is unfolding exactly as it ought to" answered Freya.

The four of them erupted into hysterical laughter.

A week had passed. No-one had mentioned Keith again, and no one had seen or mentioned Roger Parkinson either. For most of the residents, it was as if their movement to a different universe had facilitated the subtle erasure of their ever having existed in Sedgewood.

A few people noticed of course. Joy for one. Joy had fancied Keith since they'd been at school together. She used to flirt outrageously with him whenever he came into her shop. She didn't seem to mind his little quirks either, like the way he would eye up the other shoppers sometimes, the female ones that was. Keith was the best customer for the top shelf magazines too. Joy didn't mind, everyone had their little secrets. Despite the way she gossiped to everyone, she had one or two secrets herself.

Linda from the taxi-hub was concerned too. She'd had to walk into town and collect Keiths car. It had been obstructing the front of the rank. From the chit-chat between drivers on the radio, Linda soon realised that nobody else seemed especially concerned that Keith had vanished. He still hadn't come back. Linda had been feeding his Corn snake, Kellog, and was quite certain that no one else had been back to his grubby flat during the last week. Perhaps she ought to tell the police?

Norma Parkinson hadn't wasted any time at all. She'd had a locksmith visit by lunchtime on the first day of Rogers absence. She'd dug into her savings and now all the locks had been changed and the doors and windows had all had a thorough security overhaul.

Then she went onto a Dutch website she'd found on the dark-web and ordered herself a taser.

Roger was never going to set foot in that house again.

While she waited for the express courier to arrive, she'd had a good look through some of Rogers papers. The utter bastard had been claiming rent allowance and an unemployment benefit payment.

He'd been drawing out cash from the post office too. There was a drawer full of notes in the sideboard. No wonder he could afford all the high-tech computer equipment. He'd never offered her a single penny.

Norma calculated what he'd cost her in food and heating and deposited the bulk of the notes into her own account the next day.

She then asked Matt and Karen, her local 'We've got a van' team, to transport all of Rogers belongings back to her brothers grotty little caravan where it still sat on the edge of town with only two thin strands of barbed wire between it and Bobby Bunces slurry pit. She'd paid them with the last of Rogers money and included a generous tip.

The only other people in Sedgewood who noticed Rogers disappearance, were the police. They often saw Roger sneaking around at night and generally being furtive. The trouble was, until someone reported an incident, there wasn't much they could do to interrupt his peculiar nocturnal meanderings.

Over recent months, Roger Parkinson had become much better at not getting caught, and so his trips to the police station had become less frequent.

PC Dan Rapier had been involved in the leisure centre investigations. Just like Roger, he liked to know where certain people were. To date, Roger hadn't done anything to demonstrate he was dangerous, but Rapier was thorough, he didn't like loose ends, and he didn't trust anyone with Roger Parkinsons background.

Perhaps 'MI5 Roger' was hacking into other people's computers again rather than creeping around the streets at night? Rapier would see what came up after the weekend and then go and make some discreet enquiries.

Miranda hadn't gone to the market today; she had a deadline to meet. What she really would have liked. Was to have spent a little time in her favourite city doing a spot of people watching. She was looking through her diary attempting to plan ahead. Her interactions and travels were the best possible source of material to incorporate into her pieces. Miranda loved Bath, as did Sam, but at this time of year he had so many seedlings sprouting, that she knew it would be impossible to separate him from his greenhouse and poly-tunnels, even if it was only for a single weekend.

It was their wedding anniversary tomorrow and it was highlighted in red. Miranda had arranged for Nigel to spend the evening with Dan Rapier, the copper. 'Quick-as-you-like' as he'd been known since school, had a springer from the same litter Nigel had arrived with. Kevin was a little smaller than Nigel, but in every other way they were almost identical, certainly in terms of dogsonality. Sometimes Sam and Miranda would look after Kevin, and sometimes Nigel would stay with Dan. The two springers always had a great time when they got together.

Miranda had just picked up her phone to ask Dan what time to drop Nigel off, when the doorbell rang.

"Oh god." She groaned "Who the hell is it this time? Go and see will you?" She nodded to Nigel who obediently trotted out of the office and into the hall where he woofed twice.

At least that meant it wasn't Roger. Miranda got to her feet and sighed in resignation. Both she and Sam hated unexpected guests, or phone calls, or intrusions of any sort actually. This had only happened since they'd gone past their respective fortieth birthdays. Prior to that, they'd lived on flexibility and spontaneity. They'd been no strangers to late night parties, unplanned curry evenings and all sorts of impromptu gigs and excursions.

These days they liked their routines, and the doorbell ringing was always an interruption.

Two beaming faces greeted her as she opened the door. She knew their game the instant she spotted the bundle of The Lookout magazines poking out of the older ladies straw bag.

"We're talking to people today about our friend, The Lord Jesus Christ. Do you have a minute?" Before Miranda could respond, the younger woman jumped in with "Is Jesus your friend too?"

Miranda took a deep breath. Now then, would she deliver her usual speech or an abrupt "I'm busy" while swiftly closing the door again? It was too late; Nigel had slipped past her and was now making friends with the two women. 'Sabotaged, ruddy traitor.' thought Miranda. Nigel was willing to make friends with almost anyone if he thought there might be a biscuit hidden away in a pocket somewhere. The doorstep stalkers knew this too, and they'd come prepared with pockets full of gravy bones.

Miranda glanced up and down the street to witness this was a full-scale assault today. There were smartly dressed representative of what Miranda called 'The Deluded,' on doorsteps on both sides of the road. Poor Jenny had been lured out over at number 11, she caught Miranda's eye and lifted her hand to wave meekly in a gesture that said, 'Help

Me?'

Colin at number 7 was out too. He was obviously on nights and hadn't appreciated being disturbed. The note on his gate expressed his feelings clearly, but the righteous fanatics had decided they knew better.

Colin was audibly making full use of every Saxon word in his vocabulary.

Dear old Martin, the retired English teacher, had been caught as well. These people must have really put some work into their reconnaissance to get everyone at the same time. He was looking like a rabbit caught in the headlights and kept glancing around from neighbour to neighbour quietly appealing for someone to rescue him.

Miranda, who had spiritual leanings but definitely not religious ones, cast her eyes skyward and sent out the silent broadcast "Heaven help us."

She couldn't believe her luck as the clinking dangly tune of Greensleeves came to her ears, and as if by magic, the ice cream van arrived.

There were frenzied glances between all the trapped neighbours and then a swift, almost telepathic consensus. "Oo mustn't miss the van. Nigel loves ice-cream don't you Nigel?"

The two women on the doorstep didn't know how to counter this. The script they worked from covered all sorts of eventualities, but Ice cream vans hadn't been covered in the training.

"Sorry ladies, another time perhaps? Come on Nigel." The happy springer stepped obediently back inside. He understood more than enough to realise he was about to score a vanilla cornet.

Miranda stepped back, closed the door, and dashed into the kitchen for her purse. As one, her neighbours picked up on the cue and moved to find their own money. In less than 90 seconds, a queue of residents had gathered at the window of the van and were taking turns in placing their orders.

"We need to get a new ring-round sorted then." Suggested Suzie from number four on the corner. In the past, her house had always been targeted first, then she would alert everyone else on an emergency group text message.

"I reckon they must have sussed us out, just look at them all?" She continued.

Bewildered evangelists looked sadly to each other. The residents had outwitted them again. They'd have to work on a fresh strategy. They began to drift away from the doorsteps they'd been occupying.

"Probably going back to their lair" Said dressing-gown clad Colin.

There was audible chuckling as the faithful drifted dejectedly away.

As promised, Nigel was rewarded, Miranda had a flake *and* a fudge in hers. The neighbours chatted for a few minutes and then order restored, they made their ways back to their respective homes.

Miranda sat back down at her desk, thoroughly distracted from the task she'd been occupied with. Now then, how could you block an entire religious faction? She was far too agitated to get any work done. Perhaps if she just worked through her thoughts, she could find the peace to write again? It usually worked.

She sighed heavily and sat back in her chair so she could fully enjoy the fantasy.

Miranda had practised meditation for many years now and was well-practised at filling her visualisations with detail.

As it happened, at that exact moment, the congregation was gathered for debriefing in the spanky new shed which they now used as the meeting hall for the Eternally Confused. For the first time in months, there was no absenteeism. Elder Bernard had taken the register and for the first time ever, it showed a complete little column of ticks.

The group was relatively new and had been the creation of Clive and Marlene Puddle.

Clive and Marlene had taken their inspiration from the founder of another organisation who'd famously said, "If you want to get rich, then start a religion."

Clive and Marlene had experimented with several different businesses in the past, without much success. Undeterred though, they'd continued attending marketing seminars until one weekend on their way home from a particularly motivating manifestation conference in Sandy Balls, their exhaust had fallen off.

They were a long way from anywhere, but to their huge relief, emerging from the moist, foggy darkness, came a mini-bus full of happy passengers on their way home from a trip to the seaside with their local church.

One of the singers happened to know a thing or two about

cars. A roll of Gorilla tape was produced and in no time at all, Clive and Marlene were heading home again.

Clive had commented on what a smart new minibus the group had been travelling in. All bought and paid for they told him conversationally, no monthly payments on *their* bus, they'd purchased it with donations to the church. Tax free donations.

Clive and Marlene had discussed the potential long into the night as they drove back to Sedgewood.

The following day, they'd begun their research in earnest. It wasn't long until they'd discovered what recruitment strategies worked best and what tactics different factions used to both extract money from, and to keep their followers compliant.

Clive made a study of subliminal programming. Together they'd studied a whole range of other coercive techniques, like the ones used by self-proclaimed pick-up artists.

Twelve months on, Clive and Marlene Puddle had started to attend Sedgewood's main church.

They began attending the evening bible circle too. Clive joined the church football team. Marlene had even signed up for the ladies synchronised swimming group. Soon they were members of every church gathering they could fit into their schedules.

It was only a short step then to hosting meetings at their house.

Several months passed quietly, and then Marlene began having visions.

A new faith had been born, and so far, Marlene and Clive were doing rather well out of it.

Miranda focussed on her breathing.

She pictured a birds eye view of the meeting hall down by the bridge. Looking through a few wisps of cloud she could see fine silver threads of the committed running from all over Sedgewood and into the beating heart of their exclusive society.

Oh! She hadn't expected that. Mandy and Arthur from the pet-shop were there. Golly! And that nice young woman who'd been delivering her mail for the last few weeks. Oh well, never mind. It was just a fantasy anyway. It wasn't as if she could *really* block people.

She allowed her mind to paint in a few more details. Apparently, the faithful genuinely did practise deployment and recruitment strategies, with virtually military precision. Well now, she'd certainly joked about it, but here it was right before her eyes. 'Tut' she told herself 'You know you're making it all up.' Or was she?

She decided to pull all the silver threads inwards towards the hall. Nearly forty tiny figures were pulled into the gleaming white building.

Miranda made a mental note to close all the doors. The doors in her vision obliged.

Then she overlayed the whole picture with the big red hexagonal button. She reached out with her mind and pushed.

There was a distant but satisfying flushing sound.

Miranda allowed herself a few minutes to enjoy the peaceful feeling that now enveloped her and fell promptly asleep.

Roger Parkinson had very quickly adjusted to his new environment. The first couple of days had been rough, and then he'd decided, he must be in some sort of waiting room on his way to heaven.

The holographic construct, as he thought of it, had some unusual properties.

At first, he'd gone back to his sister's house. He still called it that even though he'd tried to dominate her and take over. Bizarrely, by the time he got there, none of his keys would work. He'd had to find somewhere else to sleep. He'd kept his head down on the journey, but it had become increasingly apparent that there just wasn't anybody else there other than a single taxi which he'd dived behind a laurel hedge to avoid. The sound of the taxi had quickly faded, and he hadn't heard it anywhere nearby since.

Inside the hologram, anywhere he already knew was exactly as he remembered it. He'd let himself into several houses he'd already explored. The furnishings were all there, and where previously he'd poked around in wardrobes and drawers, the contents were the same. If he came across a book or magazine he'd read, the pages were full of print and images. He was poking around inside the vicarage when he spotted a small bible lying on an occasional table. He'd never been able to get beyond Genesis on his attempts to study. He wondered if he might find something relevant now? Most of the pages were blank. There were random passages erratically dispersed among the pages which sounded familiar, but aside from Genesis, the only part which contained any significant body of words was

Revelations. He put the book back where he'd found it. The vicar had an eclectic collection of theological books. Roger decided to examine some of these. In virtually every case, the pages were blank.

He carried on exploring the bookcases, fascinated. The vicar had also been a lover of science fiction. The Long Earth series was there, and one of Rogers favourites, The Cosmic trilogy. He was delighted to discover that these tomes contained the complete transcripts.

It gradually dawned on him that anything he'd already read was here, but most of the other books contained nothing but blank pages. Perhaps he was dreaming then? Could it be that he was in a coma? Or perhaps this was a set up like the one Patrick McGoohan had found himself in when he was The Prisoner?

On the bottom shelf was a collection of children's books. The Gruffalo, The Tiger who came to tea, The Very Hungry Caterpillar and around a dozen more. Given that Roger Parkinson was in his late fifties, most of them hadn't been published until after his thirtieth birthday, yet here they were, just as he remembered them. Roger had always loved the Gruffalo.

He'd been sleeping in a cell at the police station. The local police had always behaved as if his 'mission' was just a funny little quirk. Roger had mostly gone along with it. He'd visited the station numerous times over the previous few years. Generally while handcuffed.

Now there was nobody around to criticise him, Roger had gone fully 'Tactical,' and he currently had a pair of the same handcuffs tucked into his army copy utility belt. He'd been gradually accumulating anything he felt might be useful from all over Sedgewood, and then squirreling it away in the interview room. There was quite a lot of camo-gear going on.

Food had been interesting. The shops were all full of the usual stock, there was milk and fresh bread and fruit on the shelves. None of these items, he noticed, had any use by dates, and on further inspection, neither did anything else. On day five he'd realised that some time while he slept, anything he'd taken from a shop the day before, had been mysteriously replenished. Roger had been living on banana milk and Jaffa cakes for a week now.

Rogers Spirit guide had gone with him to Blocked world. It was his first time as a Guide, and he hadn't really been away from the Earth Plane for very long himself. He'd been an actor in the last life, now he was simply Norman. He didn't need to use his former surname at all here, which was ironic, as Wisdom was what his charge was supposed to be seeking. Norman kept checking back with the boss who'd reassured him that both he and Roger were doing just fine, and that everything was unfolding exactly as it should be.

Norman wasn't entirely convinced. He wasn't entirely sure he liked Roger very much either, but he did his best to hide it, and anyway, so far Roger hadn't asked for anything. At least this scenario wasn't boring Norman thought to himself. Just imagine being a Spirit guide to a Tibetan monk? All they did was sit around meditating all day. How mind numbingly dull. Norman turned his attention back to his charge, what on Earth...no, not Earth he checked himself, what on Blocked World, was that weirdo up to now?

Roger thought he'd heard a car in the distance once or twice, but it never came close to anywhere he was. Roger had never learned to drive himself, and it was years since he'd ridden a bicycle. Leaving Sedgewood to explore the nearest village never occurred to him. Rogers world had always been Sedgewood, and it was a world he knew intimately.

For the time being, he had the whole place to himself, apart from that mystery taxi. All the better to get his research done. And if anyone else did turn up? He'd have to think about that when it happened.

For some strange reason, he could read a selection of car magazines although he couldn't remember ever having looked at one before.

It was a shame that none of the televisions worked, but he had discovered he could play DVDs. At the moment, he was working his way through all the police DVD's of their interviews with him. He glowed with pride. They'd never cracked him. They just thought he was some sort of nut job. Very-very secret agent Roger Parkinson of MI5, seconded to MI27, knew differently!

Keith had been having a similar experience regarding food and books and televisions.

Water flowed from the taps, the lights worked, there was gas to cook with, and his pound coin metre had stopped demanding to be fed. Kellog was there and appeared to be fine.

Other things were definitely not fine.

Keith had been busy exploring too, desperately hoping to find another breathing human being, preferably female. He learned he could easily enter places he already knew, but in many cases, although the outside of a building might look exactly the way he was accustomed, inside would just be an empty shell.

Some of the buildings contained things he'd expected to find, and then held a confusing selection of totally empty rooms, and then there were one or two buildings down by the river which he'd never been in at all, but where he could clearly see furniture and personal items through the windows. Mrs Buchanan's house for instance.

Without them realising, what either had experienced individually, now, they both could. This was their own unique consensus reality.

Roger tended to stick to what he knew and hadn't quite discovered this yet. Keith was struggling to understand the rules of reality in this strange place.

Worst of all for Keith, was the urge to just get away from it all, to fill the taxi up with fuel, which he'd done once, and to drive out of town and keep going until he found someone. Something was stopping him though, fear. What if he got to the edge of town and nothing else existed? Like that film from the 1980's, the thirteenth floor? In the end, the characters had discovered to their horror, that they weren't real humans, they were simulations themselves.

Keith had only watched that the week before, and the memory was crispy fresh and terrifying.

When the entire congregation of the Church of the Eternally Confused arrived in Blocked World, both Keith and Roger were completely unaware. There was a short succession of soft plopping noises. Neither of them knew it yet, but the detail in their world had just expanded substantially.

The wedding anniversary dinner had been delicious, unfortunately, Miranda had been rather distracted ever since they'd dropped Nigel off.

'Quick as you like' had welcomed Nigel and then the two spaniels had leapt away to chase one another around the orchard.

"Much going on then?" Sam had asked. The most outrageous thing to have occurred in Sedgewood recently was when Bob Onions, one of the other local vegetable growers, had been ticketed for driving at 53 miles an hour in the forty zone. The incident had been in both local papers and Bob had moved away to Shillingford very soon after.

Occasionally a stumbling drinker would be stopped by the police and ordered to return the pint glass they were clutching, to the pub it had just been 'borrowed' from. The only real news for years had been the peculiar case of Roger Parkinson's activities in the leisure centre. Consequently, when Dan answered, "I think we might have either one, or even two missing persons actually." Sam didn't know what to say.

"Can you tell us who?" Miranda had asked. That taxi driver instantly sprang to mind. In a small town, it wouldn't be difficult to find out anyway. Dan remained discreet though. "Until we know for certain, I can't comment I'm afraid."

"Ah, fair enough." Sam had answered. Miranda wanted to know more but had decided not to press the issue. "One of us will be here for Nigel first thing Monday. I'm here until Thursday next week, so we can have Kevin for a few hours on Tuesday and Wednesday if he'd like that?" She'd told their friend.

"I expect he'd like that very much. By the way, I've left something for you at the Wizards Staff, enjoy, and happy anniversary!" He stuck his hand out to first clasp Sam's firmly, and then he gave Miranda a hug and a peck on the cheek.. "You two had better get going, you'll be late."
Sam and Miranda exchanged glances. Obviously, Dan knew that some of their friends would have gathered to surprise them.

Dans gift had been a bottle of champagne. When Miranda had first arrived in Sedgewood, Dan, like half the men his age in the town, had fancied Miranda. In more recent times, both Miranda and Sam had wondered whether Dan now fancied Sam. He'd gone through a phase when the boys were puppies, when he'd suddenly begun spending a lot of time with Sam. Two years previously, he'd even turned up at a gig dressed in almost identical gear one evening. Everybody present had been uncomfortable that night. Tim had even nudged Sam a couple of times and winked at him saying "Looks like you've pulled mate."
While gesturing towards Dan.
Miranda had written an article titled 'What to do when your ex fancies your partner.'
It had gone out in the magazine, and her blog and on her website. Things had reverted to the way they'd been before the puppies, and they were all a lot more comfortable in one another's company again now.

The evening ought to have been wonderful. Tim had closed off the dining area, but it was packed anyway, mostly by friends who'd been at their wedding. There had been multiple hugs and congratulations. Tim had even made a short speech to thank everyone and wish the happy couple even more prosperity and happiness.

Sam was happy, animated, and lubricated with champagne and cider.

Miranda, meanwhile, did her best to put on a good show, but couldn't get what might have happened to Keith off her mind. Who could the other missing person possibly be? They drank, they dined, they danced and then at 11pm, the taxi Miranda had booked to take them to Sedgewood's little hotel had arrived.

Later, as Sam snored softly in the luxurious embrace of the hotel linen, the incident at the back door came back to Miranda abruptly. 'Oh my god' she gasped quietly in the darkness. Roger Parkinson!

The congregation of the Church of the Eternally Confused began to explore their new environment.

After the debriefing session, they'd sung a few songs and Marlene had taken to the rostrum to read an account of her latest vision, which was titled 'What to expect in Heaven.'

Marlene and Clive had spent hours on You-tube listening to accounts of near-death experiences.

Marlene had kept repeating the word Blissful.

Tea and cake had followed, then the meeting had broken up and the members had headed back to their homes.

It hadn't been long at all until the new arrivals in the alternative version of Sedgemoor, had begun spotting some of the anomalies.

The absence of cars and people was the most obvious.

There had been other clues too though. The phones were all silent, there were no aeroplanes flying overhead and no trains rattling along the little branch line which served Sedgewood either.

The ambient noise levels were so low, frogs could be heard croaking contentedly from ponds and water features in the gardens. Even the dragonflies sounded noisy.

One of the most noticeable things was the clarity of the air. It smelt wonderful. Jasmine and Azaleas which usually gave off only wafts of perfume, now filled the air with their potent and delicious aromas.

One of Clive and Marlene's commandments had been. "You must not fraternise with church members outside the church." If anyone ever became suspicious of them, they'd need to control the flow of dialogue. They'd told their followers that the reason was so that no inter-church infidelities could occur.

From the day they'd opened the meeting hall, Clive had set up a screen with a film showing continuous scenes of beautiful countryside from all over the world.

Unknown to the congregation, the images were interspersed with messages, one of which was 'Give generously and without question.' Another had been 'Obedience at all times.'

It served them well now. The flock had taken on all the programming, and they didn't have a clue what had been done to them.

Bewildered congregation members spread to the extremities of the little town trying to make sense of what had occurred, but none of them engaged in conversation with anyone else they came across. They just nodded politely, gave one another puzzled looks, and then went on their respective ways.

Several of them went to Sedgewood's little police station. The door was locked, and no-one answered.

Inside a soundproofed cell, Roger Parkinson was sleeping off his latest feast, surrounded by Jaffa cake wrappers and empty banana and strawberry milk bottles.

Keith was unconscious too. He'd decided that the only way to cope with this strange, whatever it was, was alcohol. Keith had never been a fan of alcohol and although he had access to every bar in town, hadn't known where to begin. He'd gone to his mums house. Everything that belonged to her was there. There was even a packet of menthol cigarettes next to her chair in the lounge. What was absent were all the smells he usually associated with home. Chip fat, burnt toast, cigarette smoke and the distinctive aroma of Avon face powder. Keith felt guilty. He hadn't been to see her since mother's day, and now, along with everyone else, she was gone. He helped himself to a bottle of sherry from the sideboard. In between slurps, he allowed himself a few tears. When he'd finished the sherry, he started on the cherry brandy. That had been at 10am. It was 6pm now, and Keith was oblivious.

Clive and Marlene had no idea anything had changed yet. They'd stayed in the Meeting Hall and were in the comfortable little lounge they'd had built for themselves. They'd probably spend the night there; they often did on a Friday. Once they finished counting the donations, they'd sit and plan the next stages of how to increase their following.
Later they'd do their kinky thing in front of the alter to the sound of their favourite Mötley Crüe album.

Most of the frightened congregation had assembled back at the meeting hall early the next morning. The strangeness was upsetting everyone now. Marlene would have the answers they reassured one another. Her channellings were indisputable.

Whenever a new member had joined the church, generally within a week, Marlene would ask for a private meeting. In the little, carefully soundproofed room, she would disclose all sorts of personal details about her subjects extended family and pass on messages about what those who had passed over, had to say to their relatives about how to complete their lives purpose.

This always meant handing a generous donation to the newly founded church. They could all continue their Great Work together.

So far, nobody had realised that Marlene was working mostly off information gleaned from Tracemyfamily.com and a quick trawl through the archives of the Sedgewood Gazette.

While Marlene was keeping the latest victims occupied, Clive would visit their homes and plant white duck feathers he'd bought on eBay. Any open window would do, or through the letter boxes. He'd also squirt particular brands of aftershave or perfume in. It didn't seem to matter whether he had the right one, the results were beyond his and Marlenes expectations.

"I could smell dad when I got home" people would say and then proudly hold up a white feather and declare "Look, I had this, it's a sign!"

Marlene and Clive discouraged their new-found followers from discussing their 'unique' experiences with one another, saying such things were intimate and ought to remain private.

Marlene and Clive hadn't expected to be so rudely awoken. "I can hear voices" Marlene had said. She pulled back the quilt and leaving Clive on the bed-settee, went to peek out of the window.

From the dim light and busy birdsong, it was only just after dawn.

"Clive, we'd better get dressed, and quickly, it looks like we've got about half the disciples outside." There was no mistaking the urgency in her voice. "What? What time is it anyway? What on earth are they doing here? Oh god Marlene, do you think we're been rumbled?" Clive was panicking.

He pulled himself up into a seated position and asked "Can you see Cathy and Malcolm Turner? No one else has got keys except them."

Marlene peeked out again "Hmm, don't think so. Thank goodness for that, oh hang on a minute, I think that's their car coming down the lane now"

Clive was fully upright now and reaching for his trousers. "I'm glad we packed everything away last night" he panted "Let's just stick to our usual and see what they have to say?"

Marlene was rummaging in her bag for a fresh blouse. "Righto, it'll be alright, they probably just saw a shooting star or something."

"Or maybe the aliens have landed and it's all over the TV?" Marlene had never heard Clive sound so nervous before. Then again, there was an awful lot at stake here. They continued their frantic dressing as they heard the main doors being unlocked from outside.

It was several minutes until they emerged from the little annex, by which time, almost everyone who'd been in the little parking area outside, had filtered through the doors. A dozen anxious conversations were taking place.

The babble was increasing in volume to a hysterical crescendo.

"…didn't see a single moving car."

"The phones are all off and so are the telly's."

"And the computers" someone else had chimed in.

"There's not a soul at the police station, we waited outside for hours."

Back in his cell, Roger Parkinson was still snoring.

From the little room they'd built as an office, Clive set the subliminals on the nature scenes to calming, and then with Marlene by his side, went amongst their flock to hear the tales of strangeness in town. While the tales were told, the last few members of the congregation arrived with tales of their own. One thing was quite clear, apart from the followers of the Church of the Eternally confused, there was nobody else in Sedgewood.

Leaving their flock in the safety of the hall to pray, Clive and Marlene set out to investigate for themselves.

The sun shone brightly, the stream chuckled quietly to itself, the ducks quacked happily, and the air was full of the sound of busy bees and the seductive scents of blossom. It was in every way, the perfect day. They went as far as the end of the road, and swiftly returned to the hall.

Clive and Marlenes temporary Spirit guides watched. Caligula had called on them to take over for a short while, so that he and Mata Hari could go and discuss their assignment with the Boss.

The Spirit guide formerly known as Prince took a long pull on the roll up he'd been smoking. "Do you think we ought to give them some clues?" he gestured through the ether to

Blocked World.

Marylin Monroe looked back with a puzzled expression. "Oh my, I don't think so. That would spoil all the fun!" There was a quiet "Ah-hem" beside them. They turned to King Neptune who had just joined them.

"Oh Hi Neppy" Marilyn greeted him warmly "What brings you here?"

"I've been asked to represent the followers guides" he answered, "Bit like a union rep."

Prince thought about this for a minute and then offered "Well mate, we could all work together, but I don't know what good it would do unless they all ask for the same thing at exactly the same time."

"Yes I know." Neptune nodded "But you have to admit, this is a novel one isn't it? Nothing in the brief said anything about this sort of thing happening."

Marilyn, who'd overseen several lives now, offered her insight. "Oh Neppy, dearest, this is what being a good Guide is all about. You know, challenges."

"Hmm" Neptune frowned. "I'm only on this one because it was Gandhi's day off when Malcolm Turner reincarnated. It was supposed to be a favour just for his first day, and then flippin Mahatma said he was busy at some party or other over on level nine."

"Oh dear, that's not like Ghandhi" Prince shook his head.

"No" Marilyn agreed "That's not like him at all." And then added wistfully "I did hear that Joan of Arc was having a bit of a shindig on her cloud. I'd have liked to have been at that one myself"

The trio heard a voice coming to them across the firmament. It was the boss.

" OI! YOU THREE!... EVERYTHING IS UNFOLDING…"

"Exactly as it ought to." Answered Neptune, Prince, and Marilyn in unenthusiastic harmony.

Miranda had barely slept. The long, dark hours seemed to elongate as she kept replaying her thoughts from the incident with Roger, subsequently blocking him, and then blocking Keith.

She knew that Dan Rapier would be up early with the boys. She had it on good authority that when Nigel stayed overnight, Dan would take both spaniels to the little café by the market square for breakfast. Nigel and Kevin were such regular visitors that now, they had their own special plates.

Dan would take them for a good run around Sedgewood's disused airfield first, and then they'd all go for plates loaded with bacon, sausages, black pudding, eggs, and toast. Word had spread in the little town, and special dog breakfasts had caught on as a result of their presence.

At last 5am arrived and the first whisps of daylight began to tiptoe around the edges of the curtains. Miranda slipped quietly from beneath the duvet and glided with the grace of a ballerina into the bathroom. She needn't have worried; Sam could sleep through an earthquake once he'd decided to switch off. As someone who always slept so lightly herself, she envied him that. She showered quickly and hurriedly towelled herself off before dressing. Hopefully, she could slip out and return before Sam stirred. If her suspicions were correct, explaining her thoughts was a chasm she hadn't begun to consider the enormity of crossing. At this stage, it was probably best to say nothing she reasoned.

She jotted down a brief message on the hotel stationary just in case Sam woke.

'Back in a minute, gone for more teabags…if I can find anyone. xxx'

The door clicked loudly behind her as phone in hand, she exited the room.

Down in reception, the hotel was already coming to life. A party of visitors had asked for an earlier than usual breakfast and consequently, despite the unsociable hour, there were already murmurings of conversation emanating from the dining room.

It was still too early to ring Dan she thought, so she sent him a brief text.

'Hi Dan, I know it's early, but can you give me a ring please?'

Next she took a seat herself and asked for a pot of tea.

The young waitress had detected Mirandas obvious discomfort and asked, "Is everything okay with your room madam?" as she'd jotted down the order.

"Everything's lovely thanks" Miranda had replied and then hoping to negate any further questions

added, "It's a lovely room, but you know how it is, I always wake up early when I'm away from home."

Miranda began investigating social media sites as she waited. Roger Parkinson didn't have any pages under his own name. Miranda searched and found several references to him on one of Sedgewood's community pages. Without exception, they all mentioned him in the most uncomplimentary tones. Some were witty, most had been written in anger. Roger Parkinson was anything but popular. She'd read through a couple of dozen posts when she came across a reference to Sedgewood duck-pond-

and-park webcam. Apparently, this was on Rogers regular route to and from his home and so it partially documented his frequent nocturnal wanderings. Roger, the author had explained, liked to keep the same routine seven days a week.

This for Miranda, was an absolute gem. She noted the times and found the link for the live feed. Was there anyway she could access the footage from the previous week?

She was delighted to learn she could access the archive material going back three months. Whoever would have thought she'd actually be glad to observe creepy Roger?

Over the next twenty minutes, with little success she attempted to sift through the webcam history. She needed to get home to where she could access a larger screen and find the time intervals more easily.

Roger in that case, would have to wait.

Next she had to search for Keith. She couldn't find him at first, but of course, she'd blocked him not just with the big red imaginary button, but also here in the real world, or at least the world of electronic wizardry.

A thought flashed through her mind, what would happen when she unblocked him? Would he suddenly turn up? She immediately dismissed the notion. She was just being daft anyway…wasn't she?

Keiths settings were set to public. His posts were as sleezy as his personality she quickly decided. Obviously between jobs, Keith had had plenty of time to peruse the full glory of the internet. Mostly though, he'd chosen to re-post items on cars and scantily clad young women, sometimes up to ten a day.

Keith hadn't posted anything since last Friday morning, just before Miranda had blocked him both on-line, and with her imagination button as she was now beginning to think of it. Her phone began to vibrate, it was Dan. She rose to her feet and began heading out to the carpark. This needed to be a private conversation.

"Hi Dan, thanks for calling, are the boys okay?" Miranda did her best to keep her tone normal.

"Yes they're having a lovely time thanks. What troubles you at this hour though? You don't usually need a check in. Is everything okay?"

Miranda had been wracking her brain for hours about how to say what followed.

"I heard about the taxi driver, Keith. Is he one of the missing people by any chance? It's just that he kept trying to talk to me and he makes my skin crawl. Between you and I, I think half the women in town found him a bit sleezy."

"Sorry Miranda, you know I really can't comment about our cases, but go on?"

Dan knew the best way to learn was to lead rather than question.

"It's just that I felt like he was stalking me. Sorry Dan, I know it's Sunday and you're not working."

Miranda could hear Kevin and Nigel barking playfully in the background somewhere.

"Oh. Well that's not good. Did you want to make it formal Miranda?" Dan had now switched to his policeman voice. It was a subtle change, but Miranda noticed immediately.

"Oh no, I don't think that's necessary, I just wondered, that's all."

"It's only just six o'clock." Dan pointed out "That's early even for you. Did you want to have a proper chat? Is everything okay with you and Sam?"

"Oh yes, yes fine thanks, we're good. Oh yes, and thanks so much for the champagne last night too. You're a sweetie Dan."

Miranda paused while she did her best to appraise how to go forward. Dan paused at his end too. The silence was an uncomfortable one. Miranda gave in first.

"It's just that he sent me a friend request last week and I blocked him. Then I heard he'd just vanished and after what you said last night, I've been wondering what happened to him."

Dan made a mental note. Why would Miranda be concerned about Keith the Taxi? Certainly, his standing among the ladies in the community was no surprise to Dan. Sleezy Keith had been mentioned on many occasions.

"Have you had any other contact from him by any chance? You know, texts, phone calls, emails?"

"Oh no, none of that." Miranda answered, "Although I did feel like he used to time getting out of his car to stretch his legs whenever I walked past the rank."

Dan had heard that statement before too. Both his sister and his ex-wife had made exactly the same remark. He'd also heard it from some of the young WPC's who used to come to Sedgewood for their induction training.

"Hmm, okay. Well I don't think really there's anything we could follow up there Miranda, unless there's anything I need to know of course? After all, anyone can send anyone a friend request."

Miranda desperately wanted to ask whether Roger Parkinson was the other missing person. She had visions of immediately being led away to the police station in handcuffs for interrogation.

It was time to end the conversation before she incriminated herself. Another part of her brain whispered to her. 'This is ridiculous. You can't just make people vanish by blocking them!'

"Oh well, not to worry, I was just awake early, and I wondered if that might mean anything." She tried to sound as cheerful and dismissive as she could. On the other end of the line, Dan could hear the speed of her speech. This wasn't the usual calm voice of the friend he'd known for so long. Miranda was worried.

"Not to worry then, I'll see you in the morning. Have a great time! Thanks Dan, you're a good friend."

"You have a great time too." He answered and then as he pressed the button to terminate the call, asked himself again, why would Miranda Boycott be concerned about Keith the Taxi?

Outside the hotel, Miranda cast her eyes skyward and addressed the brilliant blue quietly.

"If you're there, I really could do with a little help right now? Anyone?"

Freya and the other guides were delighted. "I think she might be getting the idea she's not alone." Offered Brown Cloud in a hopeful tone.

"Possibly." Artemis answered, "But she still hasn't grasped

the idea of being specific."

The other guides nodded in unison.

"I can see this all getting extremely complicated."
Nostradamus agreed and then, "What do you think Freya?
You're in charge after all. We're just here for when she
needs help with her skill set."

Freya thought about the situation for a few moments.
"You're certainly right about her being vague. conciseness
was one of her life plan targets? Can anyone remember the
full brief?"

"It's okay, I've got my copy here somewhere." Brown
Cloud began rummaging through his pockets. Eventually
he pulled out a battered parchment scroll which he unrolled
and then read aloud from"

"Life plan for Miranda Louise Parker, da, da, da
reincarnation date, na, na, na ,na, Hmm, minor details,
school stuff. First boyfriend…oh yes, remember that one?
Miranda and Alan Taylor." He laughed loudly.

"He was the one who'd ordered her head chopped off in
France that time wasn't he?" Artemis asked.

"Yes" Confirmed Freya, "He's the one, Alain Tailleur that
time. The Akash says they're supposed to get it together
properly in two lives time. She has to push him off a cliff in
her next one though, so this was just a bit of a warmup.
Anyway, carry on then" she gestured to Brown Cloud. He
seemed to be lost in thought for a minute and then
announced. "Well the life plan all seems in order, and she's
hit most of her targets so far."

"Go on?" Nostradamus, Artemis, and Freya had all been
briefed at the outset, but reminders were always useful.

"I'm just getting to the section on manifesting. Ah, here it is, erm…, ah yes, erm section 58C paragraph two, 'Apply the principles of string theory to create a new strand of reality.'

"Oh Bravo!" cheered Nostradamus and began clapping. The group exchanged smiles.

"Well I think she's doing brilliantly." Artemis said. There was much nodding.

"She has just asked for help though." Put in Freya "Ideas anyone?"

"I'm just here to help with her writing." Nostradamus ventured and then added "Oh and to help her when she realises she can do the clairvoyant thing too of course."

"My brief was assertiveness and encouragement with definitive action." Artemis said. "She's always struggled with really standing up for herself, like that time she was in with that Viking lot."

All the guides had access to Mirandas past lives records, and they nodded sympathetically.

Brown Cloud looked a little embarrassed now it was his turn. "Well, erm, as you know, erm, I'm just here to erm, help her with…" He paused.

Freya patted him sympathetically on the arm and said. "Yes it's okay. We all have to take a turn at health and bodily functions sometimes." Then she added "And of course, as you all know, I'm Mirandas primary, but I'm not really cut out for the Fairy Godmother stuff; I told the boss that when he paired us up. She really has done remarkably well this time round though, and mostly on her own. "Now then, we've still got a lot to get through, and she *has* just asked for help, so what shall we give her?"

Nostradamus gazed into the ether for a moment and then said.

"Well I've just had a quick look, and with what's coming up, I think it might be helpful if we gave her an *Unblock* button."
"Fabulous." Freya uttered her approval. Brown Cloud and Artemis agreed.

Miranda had gone back to the room and slipped back into bed beside her softly snoring husband. Sam's internal alarm clock would wake him anytime soon she thought, and sure enough a moment later, movement from beside her confirmed the inevitable. Sam did his customary morning stretch, blinked pink eyed and mole like at his wife, and then rolled out of bed and shuffled into the bathroom to emit the customary sequence of morning noises.

His opening gambit when he emerged again was "Do you think those French beans will be all right? I'm a bit worried they're not ventilated well enough." And then he added "I hope Nigel's having a good time. Do you think he misses us?"

"Oh Sam darling, can you give yourself just a couple of hours off? It's supposed to be romantic. "She gestured the bed beside her.

Sam looked at the floor and began to apologise.

"Sam, just come to bed."

For the next two hours, Miranda managed to forget about Roger and Keith entirely.

In Blocked world, a universe less than a hairs breadth away, Clive and Marlene Puddle were finally exploring the eerily uninhabited town their congregation had been trying to explain to them.

Once the initial melee had settled down, Saturday had passed with Clive and Marlene patiently speaking to everyone individually. They could see that the phones were dead, and the internet wasn't working either. There wasn't any traffic passing the hall, and none could be heard in the distance.

Clive was so unsettled that he'd been sneakily sipping vodka from a bottle tucked away in their private room. "Do you think this is gods punishment?" Marlene had asked later that afternoon while they took some time out in their private room. "Pass the bottle will you?"
They were both frightened by what they'd heard so far, Clive had always had a nagging suspicion that he was being watched. He might have reacted differently if he'd known it was Caligula.

Caligula had returned and he was feeling grumpy. He'd decided he was going to petition the boss and see if he could transfer to a different assignment. He'd had to stay on site while Clive and Marlene had been doing the kinky thing the previous evening, and now he was feeling quite traumatised. Mata Hari could see his point of view. There wasn't much she hadn't seen either; she was quite distressed too. The boss had said No and sent them back to get on with the job they'd been tasked with.

Marlene and Clive hadn't felt brave enough to venture out into Sedgewood further than the end of the road straight away. Just that short distance had tested their nerves. They'd have to eventually though. They'd asked their flock to return to their homes and return the next morning. "Better something happens to any of them than to either of us." Clive had said as the last few reluctant stragglers had left at what had proven to be an exceptionally long day.

As daylight broke on Sunday, they'd steeled themselves and left the safety of the hall once more.

They'd had a quick look on foot first, and then they'd gone to find their aged purple Ford Capri. Clive had never had the heart to get rid of it, and the disassembled shells of three similar vehicles now inhabited their back garden. Clive had wanted to make sure he had plenty of spares for his beloved passion-wagon. Reassuringly, the car at least was exactly where they'd left it.

They were currently driving around the town on the same circuits Clive had driven during his boy-racer days.

Several times they'd stopped to investigate shops or cafes which were usually open by now on a Sunday.

Just as Roger and then Keith had discovered, the displays were full of fresh produce, but there was nobody to be seen. Not anywhere.

They combed the streets of Sedgewood for over an hour.

Eventually, they decided to knock on a few of their neighbours doors, so they drove home and parked in their usual spot.

"You try Mavis and Brian; I'll try Mrs Roberts." Marlene had said as she gently closed the passenger door of the historic vehicle. Clive nodded and hummed in agreement. They set off in different directions. Five minutes later they were back at the car. "Nothing. Not anyone." Clive said in the same tone he used when they'd been out attempting to recruit more followers.

"How about you?"

Marlene held up her hands with a shrug. "Not one person. I even went around the back at Debbie and Thomases" she gestured towards a house a few doors along the avenue. "You'd have thought at least some of the kids would be home?" The family she referred to, had nine children, and had recently appeared in a documentary about coping with a large family. Their home was generally considered the noisiest house in Sedgewood. Today, apart from the ticking of seven different alarm clocks, it was silent.

Clive was as confused as his congregation had been. "Well, I have no idea what the hell's going on, but we'd better keep everyone on side. For now at least.
What on earth are we going to tell them?"
"I don't know." Marlene answered, "Perhaps we should drive over to Shillingborough and see what's happening over there?"
Clive thought about the idea for a minute. Perhaps they were part of one massive practical joke? Could that be possible?
"Good idea. Let's go back to the hall first and then perhaps a few of us can go out of town and see what we find?"

As they headed back to the meeting hall, Clive turned to Marlene and asked, "Have you noticed anything odd about the car?"
"Yes I have actually, it's not puffing oil is it?"
"Precisely!" Clive answered and then he tapped on the petrol indicator "And we're not burning any fuel either."
They pulled into the small parking area by the hall.
Everyone welcome the sign on the wall announced, and underneath, 'Strictly Church parking only!!!'
A sea of anxious faces greeted them on their return.
"Where is everyone?"
"What did you see?"
"Marlene, have you had any guidance from the Lord?"

The voices began to compete with one another. Clive raised his hands to try and silence his worried flock. It had the same effect as attempting to carry sand on a tennis racket.

He made his way through the congregation and mounted the podium in the main hall.

"Brothers, sisters, be at peace." Clive commanded from the pulpit while making the obedience gesture with his raised left hand.

At once, the assemble mass became quieter and gently slid into seats, just as they'd been hypnotised to do.

"Lets us pray" he commanded. His audience, again, just as they'd been programmed, clasped their hands, and lowered their heads in prayer. Clive winked at Marlene. Marlene winked back. Clive loved being in charge and Marlene loved to watch him.

He rattled through the prayer he'd specially written to reinforce his authority over the gullible.

Afterwards, as the forty faces all looked to him for his fatherly wisdom, he began his new line.

"The world has undoubtedly changed."

Despite having stated the blatantly obvious, there were approving murmurings of agreement.

"We must do as our Lord would desire of us and go and explore." More murmurings and a few yeses became audible. Fuelled by the appreciation, Clive carried on.

"For we are the flock of the eternally confused"

It was important to get that in. Marlene nodded approvingly from the doorway.

"Confusing are the ways of our sovereign."

The assembled crowd was warming up now and the

murmuring became louder affirmations.

At this point, Clive could have announced to the congregation that he was a giant chocolate penguin who loved eating custard, and they would have applauded. Instead he persevered with the direction he'd begun.

"And we embrace that confusion."

Clive and Marlene had discussed the name of their invented religious faction for weeks before settling on 'The Eternally Confused.' It had been a joke at first, but the deeper they'd looked, the more sense it made. For instance, how come this loving god the priests talked about, would send his children to a place of torment and misery at the end of their lives, like Blackpool? If god loved his flock so much, and their places of worship, why did he keep wrecking the rooves? Were roofers his favourite profession that they should have a constant source of employment? These and many other questions had been levied at the followers to demonstrate just how confusing this earthly existence was. And since yesterday, it had become even more so.

"We have been given a wonderful opportunity." Clive continued "And we have missions for all of you." He looked down over the sea of upturned faces which were beginning to look a little more hopeful now.

Clive marvelled. It really was amazing just how large a slice of the population was willing to completely abdicate responsibility for their own lives and do exactly as they were told.

Marlene began clapping and obediently, the rest of the

flock joined in.

Miranda and Sam had missed breakfast. The sun was shining brilliantly when they left the hotel. "We could go for Sunday lunch at the Riverside if you fancy?" Sam suggested as he loaded their bags into the back of the taxi. "There might even be a band on. We're child free after all." He joked.

"I bet those three are having a lovely time." Miranda answered as she climbed in. "I do miss him though. I love our boy."

Miranda wasn't kidding. She absolutely doted on Nigel. The feather eared spaniel was the only being in the universe who was allowed to interrupt her sleep without being grumbled at. He was allowed to take his time making decisions and to leave muddy paw prints everywhere, or any of the very many other indulgences especially reserved for 'His Royal Woofness.'

Nigel had a great life; Sam was just as enamoured with their brown eyed boy. Miranda didn't know it, but Sam even had screw-top jars of hot-dog sausages hidden away in his shed as treats for Nigel. Nigel loved them.

In exchange for bed and board, Nigel loved them both with absolute devotion. He would frolic to make them laugh, and when either of them felt a little poorly or low of mood, there was Nigel with his big grin, his wagging tail, and his loving companionship.

Nigel did his best to divide his time equally between his humans. When Miranda worked away she might ring home a couple of times a day. Sam had soon come to realise that she wasn't really calling to speak to him, she was checking in with Nigel.

Dan Rapier living so close and having brother Kevin, full name, Kevin the destroyer of Wellingtons, had been a godsend. Neither Sam nor Miranda could have ever considered putting Nigel in Kennels, not even for a single night. Dan's willingness to dog-sit had allowed them the freedom to have an occasional evening or weekend away. They were even considering going on holiday this year, if Sam could pull himself away from his polytunnels and vegetable plots that was.

They reciprocated frequently, and Kevin-woof as he was mostly called in their house, was as comfortable staying with his brother as he was in front of the fire at home.

The Riverside was Sam and Miranda's other favourite pub in Sedgewood. For a small town, Sedgewood was well populated with pubs and bars. The population of just under ten thousand somehow managed to keep almost thirty assorted pubs, bars, and restaurants alive. Sedgewood was a pretty little town surrounded by beautiful countryside. It had a reputation for its annual festival, and its own very distinct cheese. The biggest event of the year though, was always the historical re-enactment of 'Throwing all the town councillors into the street,' which took place on the first Friday of June every year. The annual reenactment had now evolved into a festival.

Sedgewood attracted people all year round. Competition was hot, prices reasonable, and standards high.

Some of the more zealous religious factions would sometimes focus on the town, appalled by what they considered debauchery and hedonistic decadence. On several occasions this had led to clashes between the righteous and the local troops of Morris dancers. There had been some rather unseemly handkerchief waving.

Today, the last weekend in May, was the anniversary of Rebellion day. Local people took Rebellion day very seriously. By the standards of most English traditions, it was relatively youthful. Nevertheless, those who'd been present still remembered with pride, the day the townspeople had had enough of being pushed around by a handful of local bureaucrats. It commemorated that famous weekend in 1982 when a party of disgruntled boozers, including the landlady and barmaid from the Bishops Fiddle, had decided to take matters into their own hands.

Now, to celebrate the occasion, the celebrants would dress as the pivotal figures and tour the pubs giving rousing, if a little slurred speeches, and encouraging the great Sedgewood Council tossing.

When Sam and Miranda arrived at the Riverside, things were just getting underway. Standing on a table outside and true to the events of the day, swigging from a bottle of Lambrusco, one of the many Sharon Clegg look-alikes was rousing a crowd of assorted Nick Joneses and Bobby Martins. There were shell suits and mullets in abundance. Sam had been just fourteen during the original events, which had been just old enough to sup half pints of lager and lime, as long as he stood quietly in the corner of whatever pub he was in.

Looking at all the clothing and hairstyles, he remembered it well, and the memory almost brought a tear to his eye. It was one of the reasons they'd picked that particular weekend to get married.

"You grab a table; I'll get us a drink." he suggested.
Soon they were comfortably settled a little way back from
where the band would set up, but importantly, still close
enough to get to the bar easily.
Food was selected and served, and gradually the place
began to fill with happy punters.
Food was devoured, pints were quaffed, and the ambient
noise level crept up until anyone wishing to be served had
to shout their order across the now packed bar.
When the band started to play, they barely made a dent in
the crescendo of raised voices.
The drummer of The Din-er Time looked puzzled. Not
because of anything in particular, that was his normal
expression.
The Din-er time played what they called a fusion of prog-
rock and eighties cover versions. They'd planned their set
today to commemorate the events of 1982. The noise they
made was by even the lowest standards, quite appalling.
The band was to music what atomic weapons were to art
galleries.
It was still a huge improvement on rap music though, and
the assembled crowd loved it.
What followed was an embarrassing spectacle of
reenactors, most of them in their sixties and seventies, on
their feet and getting into their rock groove as the band
smashed out classics like Physical and the classic Kenny
Rogers hit, Love will turn you around.
The third time Sam had managed to save their drinks after
some inebriant had crashed into their table, he and Miranda

had decided to continue their afternoon somewhere a little less frenetic.

As she rose to her feet, a tall man dressed unmistakably as Trevor Cooper, leered at her, sloshing lager as he lurched. "Come and have a dansh darlin." he managed to slur.

He must have spotted Miranda watching him in awed fascination a few moments previously. What he called dancing, Miranda would have described as someone having a profound anaphylactic reaction.

Miranda managed to maintain her dignity and simply replied. "No thank you. My husband and I are just leaving." Unseen by anyone, Freya leaned forward and quickly whispered something which was only audible to Mirandas subconscious.

The Trevor glanced at Sam and pulled a face "Wot? That little squirt? Come and 'av a dansh wiv a real man darlin!" Mirandas eye roll was almost as loud as the band. Despite the presence of a table between them, the Trevor attempted to grab Mirandas arm and pull her towards him. Half a dozen glasses smashed to the floor spraying sticky liquid.

Miranda jerked her arm back and then immediately beckoned the Trevor toward her.

Sam looked on admiringly. He'd seen Miranda do this once before in Paris when a man on the metro had kept surreptitiously stroking her bottom.

The Trevor complied, and before he could register his own stupidity, Miranda jabbed him straight in the eye with her fingers.

Nobody manhandled Miranda.

The Trevor's hands shot up to his face and he careered

backwards with a yelp, crashing first into the bass player, and then into the drumkit.

Sam grinned broadly at Miranda who made the blowing away smoke from a gun gesture. They left quickly, before anybody could identify them in the chaos.

"Who was that idiot?" Miranda asked as they strolled along the riverbank.

"I'm not entirely sure, but I think he might be the new vet. He's taking over from Mr Wilson in a couple of months."

"Well I definitely won't be taking Nigel to him." Miranda replied with a finality Sam knew well.

In Blocked World, or as the Guides were calling it, New Sedgewood, following the morning of investigating the town, there was no doubt in any of the congregations minds that they were alone here now.

Roger Parkinson habitually moved around at night. Nobody else had the courage to venture outside during the hours of darkness, and so far, Roger had completely evaded detection.

Keith the taxi had discovered that once he'd drained a sherry bottle, it was miraculously full again the following day. Unknown to the faithful, Keith had stayed in the safety of his mother's house and was working his way through his mother's collection of Rogers and Hammerstein musicals. Bloody Mary had sung Happy Talk and Keith had sobbed himself to sleep.

It was a reaction anyone who'd been forced to sit through the entire performance might have experienced.

The congregation were convinced they had the whole town completely to themselves.

They'd also realised that the shops they took items from seemed to magically replenish themselves, so food wasn't going to be a problem.

But what about further afield?

Caligula and Mata Hari had been watching over the painful process of Clive and Marlene's attempt to encourage their congregation to do a little more exploring.

Prince and Marilyn had made themselves scarce, having sensed the same thoughts in Caligula and Mata Hari's minds. Neptune had gone too, only in his case, he'd just disappeared, and it seemed unlikely he would return, especially now he'd been reminded about the party. Caligula had been sulking but was brought back into the moment when the questions had begun again.

"Why do we need to leave Sedgewood?" an anxious voice had asked.

"Surely Marlene has received the information we need?" asked another with trembling timidity.

Mata Hari winced.

Marlenes life plan had been to develop the ability to see through deceptions, and to be far less easily fooled herself. Now here she was spouting absolute rubbish while claiming to be channelling divine messages from the 'Seven of Heaven.'

When Marlene and Clive had been planning and plotting, both Mata Hari and Caligula had screamed at their charges not to do what they were intending. Marlene and Clive had ignored all the messages, dreams, and signs, especially the big one Mata Hari and Caligula had made together which said STOP! CONSIDER THE CONSEQUENCES! Which they'd placed right next to the traffic lights on the end of Clive and Marlenes road.

Clive had announced that he had missions for everyone, but then he'd ground to a halt. Marlene had been full of expectation too. Clive would think of something. But Clive hadn't, and the git had suggested she mount the podium to offer a few words of reassurance to the well beyond merely confused. Now they were absolutely bewildered.

Despite the lack of preparation, she'd done her best and told her audience that the messages were still a little unclear, and that she would have to seek additional guidance while they prayed for her. Afterwards, she and Clive had slipped away to confer in their tiny apartment. Around half of the Eternally Confused stayed obediently with heads bowed. The remainder went out for another look around Sedgewood. A few of those had anything less than religious intentions.

Tim Hammer and James Tong went straight to one of the pubs to commiserate. How they'd found themselves in this situation was beyond them. They'd only gone along in the first place as they'd thought the church might be a good place to pick up girls. They'd been barred from just about everywhere else. Until very recently, despite both men being in their forties, they'd lived at home with their mums. They liked football and beer, having their meals cooked by their mums, and getting their laundry done.
Their combined skill set was playing video games and generally making themselves unemployable by stubbornly refusing to be anything other than devastatingly immature. The doors of the Pickled Parson had been open.
They strode in, and Tim had stepped behind the bar and pulled them both a pint of lager and blackcurrant. James picked out a few tunes from the duke box. The opening bars of Hey Micky began pumping.
"I gotta tell you this mate." James announced over the din.
"Go on?" Tim had a few things to share himself.
"Well, you know we've been here for a bit now?"
"Yesss" Tim nodded and swallowed a mouthful of pink

bubbles, still hovering behind the bar.

"Well, you see, being as it was Saturday yesterday..."

Tim nodded again.

"It was time to change me skiddies. Mother insists I do it at least once a week" he added. Tim nodded sympathetically and belched loudly.

"Same thing in our house mate."

"Well, see, I left 'em on the floor in my room like I normally do, and this morning, they were fresh as a daisy, look!"

Before Tim could object, James had hoisted down his joggers to expose a stripe free panel at the rear of his Tigger Y-fronts. "And my Iron Maiden Tee-shirt was all clean too, and folded just like mum does it." To Tims relief, James hoisted his joggers back up again. "What do you think of that then?" He began walking back toward the bar. Now it was Tims turn.

"That's really interesting dude. I've been eating the trifle mum made, you know, just before the...the..." he paused and then finally decided on an appropriate word "...changes."

"Yeah."

"Well every night I go back to the fridge, and it's whole again, and the cream hasn't gone off or anything."

"Mazin'"

"Yeah, 'mazin. Fancy a game?" Tim indicated the pool table.

"To be honest mate, it's a bit weird, but the only thing I really miss is gaming." James volunteered, the sadness in his voice quite noticeable.

" Yeah, me too." Agreed Tim "It's just not the same with

just us two is it? Still, I like the free beer. I'm having a pint of Bailys next, fancy one?"

Louise Wattle and her girlfriend Rita Daub had joined for attention too, only in their case they'd have been better off joining 'The sisters of the eternal victimhood.'
Louise and Rita had met on a Facebook page called Empaths Only. In a collective of people who needed constant reassurance they were special, they'd found one another. In no time at all they were comparing stories about how bad things always happened to them, and how it was always someone else's fault.
It was so competitive there were times they could barely allow one another to speak.
They were oblivious that their claims to be empathic, were actually narcissistic. They were made for each other.
Neither would admit it, but both Louise and Rita thrived on immersing themselves in a good drama, and it didn't get any more immersive than this.
Before landing in Blocked World, they'd shared another trait. Either of them would steal anything if she'd thought she could get away with it. Neither's empathy had extended to the people they'd stolen from, or whose time they'd wasted, or taken advantage of for their own ends.
They'd only joined the Church of the Eternally Confused as they thought they might make some currency from it.
Both were ambitious, and right now they were cycling around the streets of Sedgewood looking for a house, a nice big one. As long as there were no other people around, then why not?
Rita came to a halt outside the front of the Old Manor

House. "How about this one?" She asked as Louise came alongside.

"Hmm, yeah, lovely int it. It's got to be the nicest house in Sedgewood any day!" Louise had always wanted to live somewhere grand; this was her chance.

"Let's go and have a look eh?"

They propped the recently acquired bikes against the garden wall and made their way up to the front door on foot.

"I reckon this'll do us nicely." Louise had already made up her mind.

"We'll have to get some sage smudge, and crystals though eh? Who knows what they used to get up to in here." Rita was already planning to strip Sedgewood's little New-Age shop bare.

Similar scenes were unfolding in half a dozen locations around their version of the little town.

The remainder of the congregation had been persuaded to arrange themselves into small groups and to go and explore the surrounding countryside.

The next nearest town was Shillingborough. That was about ten miles away. Four intrepid volunteers had agreed to go in that direction to investigate.

To the south lay Grindlebury. No one wanted to go there even when things were normal. Grindlebury was a perfect example of a post war New Town gone wrong. It was a place big corporations sent their employees to work when they wanted them to resign.

Nobody from Sedgewood would be going quite that far

today, and to everyone else's relief, it was Clive and
Marlene who drew the short straw to investigate
Grindlebury's near neighbour, Bumford.

The remaining followers divided themselves into two
groups who would travel to the villages immediately to the
east and west.

It was agreed that everyone would meet back at the hall at
7pm. With obvious anxiety, the faithful began heading
outward, first to their cars, and then onto adventures.

Sam and Miranda strolled home happily arm in arm, chatting contentedly as they walked. Miranda waited patiently twice while Sam availed himself of public toilets en route. "I don't know how you do it" he remarked as he exited the block on the edge of the park. "It's because all women have superior plumbing." Miranda had quipped and then laughed.

Secretly, she wished they were a bit closer to home. There was no way she was going to use the public lavatory; she'd seen what people did in them.

It was a beautiful sunny afternoon and people were out in their gardens mowing their lawns and trimming the rapidly growing hedges.

Miranda was looking ahead as Sam took an interest in what was flowering, and which gardens needed a little more love. Miranda pulled on his elbow and said quietly. "Can we cross over? The clique is out."

"Oh god." Sam groaned "I was hoping we wouldn't have to see any of those unbearable assholes."

Berkeley Buildings was an art deco style apartment block, built on the corner they had to turn to get onto their own road.

Sam and Miranda had lived here in a rented flat for a little while, just before they'd bought their house. Four of the flats were still rented out today.

In earlier times, the owner had used the garden as a rubbish dump, and prior to Sam's arrival, an assortment of household and builders refuse had been allowed to accumulate. As the owner had set the example, so consequently had the other residents followed. There were bottles, dead fridges and televisions, and dozens of black bags of who knows what horrors. The whole place was a paradise for rats.

Sam had worked hard to remove all the accumulated rubbish and bramble, and to then build a beautiful garden. All the residents had said how lovely it was now and had willingly accepted the surplus vegetables and strawberries that Sam offered his neighbours.
Once the work was completely finished, and the very last section had been cleared of the blackthorn and dumped mattresses and window frames, the four long-term residents had decided it was their garden. Not one of them had lifted a finger to help Sam while he'd grafted in the lashing rain and blazing sun.

Where Sam had painstakingly built and nourished a vegetable garden over four years, the leaseholders now decided to shoe-horn him off. 'It's the only bit of level ground there is' they'd told him. 'We want to put a sunbathing area there.'
It was level because he'd spent weeks of hard graft levelling it in the first place, and only after he'd asked whether anyone objected to him growing vegetables on that section. At the time, the other residents had no interest at all in the steeply sloped bramble patch.

They'd insisted he take down his polytunnel and the rainwater harvesting system he'd built, declaring that they were apartment owners, and he was a mere tenant. Sam was usually placid, but this had really got under his skin. They were all leaseholders; it was just that his was a rolling lease and theirs were longer termed ones. It was hair-splitting at its absolute worst.

Afterwards, as Sam had predicted, the area he'd cleared had once again been neglected. The bramble and bindweed had recolonised the area.

Things had become a lot more acrimonious after that. Sam had learned that one of the leaseholders, Kristen, a recent arrival in Sedgewood, had been running him down in conversations in local shops and some of Sedgewood's pubs.

In a small town, word soon got back to Sam's ears from concerned friends.

All the time he and Miranda had been making Kristen welcome, offering her vegetables and Mirandas expertise in putting a website together; Kristen had been knifing them both in the back saying things like "They're completely taking over our garden" and "When I text her with something important, she doesn't bother replying for hours. She's so rude!" Kristen neglected to mention that most of her text messages were sent at 11.45 on weeknights.

Kristen had also been helping herself to Sam's strawberries, and then giving them to her friends to curry favours. Sometimes Sam would buy boxes of books at auction and re-sell a few. Before the residue was taken to their local charity shop, Kristen had always been offered, and always accepted large quantities of these. She'd used these to curry favours too, and never once had she offered anything by way of reciprocation. Such was Kristens gift at extracting what she wanted from people; Miranda had christened her Nosferatu. Sam and Miranda had also named Kristen's boyfriend Renfield, after the character in the Bram Stoker novel. Renfield, like the character in the novel, was so enamoured, he did everything he was instructed, which included a rather frail attempt to square up to Sam on a couple of occasions.

Sam had refused to bite. Renfield had decided that Kristen was a genuine victim., after all, she'd told him in great detail about how horrible Sam and Miranda had been to her ever since she'd arrived.

Sam, normally so calm and amenable, had stewed over the revelations for weeks before saying anything. When he did, the confrontation had left no one under any illusions where they stood.

The 'discussion' had been clearly overheard by all of the residents in Berkeley Buildings. Sam had made certain of that by picking a Sunday morning when everyone had their windows open.

The response was that Kristen had gone crying to her other neighbours claiming now that she was being bullied. The neighbours had rallied around their wronged fellow leaseholder. Nobody bothered asking Sam or Miranda for their side of the story, even though they all knew their toxic neighbour was constantly trying to pitch people against one another.

She'd stirred the shit-pot, and now she'd been discovered, she was playing the role of victim.
Sam and Miranda had suddenly found themselves ostracised, which stung smartly given that it had been their intention to improve the building generally and get everyone talking to one another in the first place.

Sam, reluctantly, turned his attentions elsewhere. Within months, what had been a beautiful garden, had begun to look neglected again, and the residents were once more dumping their rubbish around the building. A defunct washing machine stood, slowly rusting at the back of the building. An old sofa appeared at the end of one of the paths. One of the residents decided to annex a section of the communal garden and promptly filled it with an assortment of unsightly debris and four dogs, transforming what had been a pretty little enclave, into a sordid looking dogs lavatory.

After they'd moved out, it was inevitable that Sam and Mirandas paths would cross those of their former neighbours. At those times, Sam simply ignored them. If he had engaged, he would probably have expressed his true thoughts, and that wouldn't have been pretty.
Miranda on the other hand, had always been approachable, and although she wanted nothing to do with them either, all four clique members continually attempted to engage her in conversation, as if they could somehow normalise what sanctimonious dickheads they'd been.

This afternoon, all four clique members were standing in

the front of Berkeley Buildings arguing about the trees. Sam and Miranda had crossed now and were hoping to avoid being spotted. The 'beastly bunch' as Miranda referred to them, had seen Sam and Miranda though, and it was too late.

The pantomime began. All four of the beastly bunch adopted postures of super niceness. Miranda did another of her audible eye rolls.

"Oh hi you two" Kristens sickly sweet voice oozed across the road. Sam and Miranda both nodded and kept walking.

"Oh hello" came the voice of dishonest Donald.

"Erm Sam? Can we borrow you a minute?" This was Alan. Alan and Sam had been friends before the clique had been established. Alan was the only one of the four Sam had any time for at all, but even that was sparse since the clique had formed.

Sam did his best to adopt a relaxed demeanour. Reluctantly, he crossed back. "What's on your mind?"

The unmistakable south London tones of Toya interrupted with "We need to cut this big purple fing back" she indicated the magnificent wisteria which grew across the front of the building "and this yellow fing gets in the way of mine and Kristens view of the river." She pointed at a laburnum Sam had planted himself. It was flowering and Sam thought it looked beautiful. When he'd planted it some years before, he'd made certain that the only view it obstructed was the electricity substation on the other side of the road.

The laburnum also had a particular sentimental value to Sam. He'd planted the original seed when he was ten years old. His father had encouraged him to look after it. He'd

nurtured the seedling, and then the sapling until finally
planting it in its final home in the front of Berkeley
Buildings, having already looked after it in a huge ceramic
pot, for fifteen years.

His father had passed away just the year before Sam had
planted it. Sam had scattered a small handful of his father's
ashes onto the root ball. Every time Sam saw the tree, in
his heart, he would feel the comforting warmth of his
father's presence.

Before he could say anything, Toya continued "I fink it
would be much better if that fing was chopped down. It
makes a right mess of my car when the flowers fall off."
She pointed again, this time to an enormous white truck
that would have been better suited to crossing an Antarctic
wasteland rather than facilitating shopping trips to
Sedgewood's market square.

"Perhaps you could come and cut it down for us?" Kristen
put in. "I know you normally charge for things like that,
but perhaps you could do it and I'll pay you back the
favour some time?"

Sam could feel his blood pressure beginning to rise.
Miranda was speechless for a moment.

"Or I could borrow your chainsaw and do it?" Alan
offered. "We're all back to work tomorrow, I don't
suppose you could drop it off could you?"

Dishonest Donald had finally found his voice.

"We could kill off that purple thing too then…" and as an
afterthought added 'mate.'

Sam's final iota of composure left him, and one at a time he looked them each in the eyes.

"You bunch of absolute fucking twats." Was all he said, and then he turned away again, and continued stomping home.

Miranda swiftly followed him, aghast at what had just taken place.

They walked in stunned silence.

Once they'd closed the front door behind them, Miranda decided it was her turn to do the pouring and headed straight to the little cabinet in the lounge. Soon she reappeared bearing a large tumbler of Irish whiskey and the bottle to replenish the equally swiftly drained glass.

During their 15 years together, the only time she'd ever seen Sam this angry was when their beloved ginger cat had been clipped by a speeding car. Mr Wilson, the vet, had managed to save Gordon, but he'd had to amputate his magnificent tail.

A full twenty minutes passed before Sam was able to speak. Miranda made a pot of tea and sat down quietly facing him, patiently waiting for him to find the right words.

"I can't believe that bunch of insincere, sanctimonious, condescending, patronising, dictatorial, self-interested, selfish, self-absorbed, moronic, lazy, infantile, duplicitous, vandalic assholes would actually have the audacity to ask me to lend them my tools, and to even drop them off for their bloody convenience." He managed at last.

"Don't hold back Sam." Miranda picked up the bottle and refilled the tumbler giving him a broad grin.

The spell was broken, and Sam's anger gave way to bewilderment. Miranda got up and walked around the table to hug him.

"I love you. They just don't know when to shut up do they? I'm amazed they still haven't learned after all this time, and I'm amazed you were so restrained with them. You're still a bit cross then?"

"A bit? Forgiveness is for people who don't understand revenge properly." Sam was joking now Miranda knew. Things would bother him, but generally he'd go out to the allotment and move compost around while muttering to himself until whatever was troubling him had worked its way out of his system.

Unfortunately, as she'd just vocalised, the beastly bunch just didn't know when to leave them alone, and the deep wound had never been allowed to properly heal.

Miranda hated seeing Sam like this. Nigel did too, and whenever one of his humans was upset, the happy spaniel would press himself up against them and offer his support and sympathy. The house felt horribly empty without his familiar reassuring presence.

Sam continued "The only reason that thick bint wants to murder that laburnum is because of her precious ruddy car."

Miranda took up the thread. "I expect Nosferatu wants it gone because she knows you planted it and knows full well that you place such value on trees."

Sam sighed and answered simply "I wouldn't be surprised."

"She's got Alan and Donald wrapped around her fingers tighter than a wedding ring. They'll just go along with anything that she wants."

"I know." Sam conceded "Poor Alan, he was a decent

bloke before she came along, I used to think he was a friend, now I just think he's a manipulable fool."

Miranda rarely heard him speak of anyone like that. He must be far more deeply hurt by the betrayal from his former friend than he'd ever vocalised.

In her mind's eye she saw the big red hexagonal button again. Her thoughts quickly drifted to the two people she'd asked Dan Rapier about just a few hours earlier.

Miranda would have done virtually anything for Sam, and at this point, if it meant the clique disappeared out of their lives altogether, whatever karma brought her as a consequence, it would probably be worth it.

As evening fell on the two Sedgewood's, two very different scenes were unfolding. In the source world, as the Guides were now referring to it, people were settling down for their last few hours of relaxation before they had to return to their hamster wheel employments in the morning.

In New Sedgewood, an animated discussion was taking place in the meeting hall for the congregation of the Church of the Eternally Confused. They were certainly living up to their chosen name.

The returning explorers had all shared the same types of experiences Roger and Keith had encountered while exploring Sedgewood.
The countryside all appeared to be unchanged. There were birds in the hedgerows and sheep grazing on the downland. There were pigs happily rooting around in the usual fields that the locals called Porklands. The little river babbled contentedly through the meadows to the east and west of Sedgewood, and the intrepid explorers had noted that there were little fish in the streams. There were rabbits and molehills, and Clive and Marlene had even seen a family of badgers crossing the road as they'd driven slowly back from Bumford. What there weren't any of, were people. There were no moving vehicles, nor trains or any aircraft flying overhead apparently.

One thing which left everyone puzzled, was that although all the other humans had vanished, their pets were all present, and there was no discernible change in them. They came across several cats going about their usual business, who didn't appear in the least little bit troubled by the absence of the humans who, presumably, fed them every day. One or two of the more observant members of the congregation deduced that the animals feeding requirements, seemed to operate on the same repeating cycle that replenished the shops with fresh loaves and fruit and pints of milk.

The biggest question in everyone's minds now though, was what was the world like outside of Sedgewood?

In Bumford, Clive and Marlene had experimented by opening a few front doors and peering inside the houses. There was nothing at all inside, no walls, ceilings, or stairs, just the external walls and the undersides of the rooves. The only place where they had found anything internal which looked normal, was the little Close of council bungalows where Marlenes Auntie Sheila had lived.

Auntie Sheila had passed away almost a decade before, and yet when Marlene had looked through the window, the inside of the little bungalow had looked exactly as Marlene remembered it, right down to the very last detail. Still present were all the horrors of 1970's décor which auntie Sheila had hung onto until she'd watched her final episode of Emmerdale.

"That's never right." She'd exclaimed to Clive.

Clive had been peering in through the windows of number three on the opposite corner. It was empty. When Auntie Sheila was alive, the rumour on the Close was that Mr Bennett had thousands of pounds in notes tucked away inside cushions and behind skirting boards. To Clive's huge disappointment, number three was as empty as some of the other shells they'd been looking at. Clive was having great difficulty coming to terms with the notion that whatever had happened, money was no longer relevant.

He crossed the road to join his wife.

"Look at that would you?" Marlene pointed through the window to a picture of a dark-haired Spanish woman with big brown eyes. It was a classic.

"Didn't your brother take that?" Clive asked even though he already knew the answer. Marlene answered with a simple 'Yep! Can we go in?' 'Hmmm' Clive stepped sideways and knocked on the door loudly. Nothing happened. In a strange way, they were both relieved. What if someone had come? What, Marlene thought with a chilling shiver, would have happened if Auntie Sheila had opened the door? Clive would have probably fainted. Marlene grasped the door handle and obligingly, the door swung open.

"Hello?"

The only answer was silence. Marlene took another sharp intake of breath and gasped "Look!" as she pointed at the row of coat hooks mounted just beside the telephone table. "Oh my." Just as Marlene had done, Clive instantly recognised Auntie Sheila's orange floral anorak. It had been her favourite, and it had special sentimental value. Auntie Sheila had always worn it when she'd gone dogging at the back of the Cash and Carry. She'd also worn it specially for when she'd been interviewed for that famous channel four programme about the more senior doggers and what motivated them.

It had been the cause of considerable discussion when

Auntie Sheila had passed. Some of the family wanted to donate it to the local charity shop. Marlene had stood her ground and auctioned it on eBay. In the end, it had made £22 and the feedback said it had been purchased by a devoted fan.

Now here it was, along with all Sheila's other outdoor gear, hanging back on its peg in the hallway.

Everything else was almost exactly the way it had been on the fateful day Clive had popped round to try and borrow some more money from his wife's auntie, and found her propped up in her armchair, eyes still open. Predictably, Doc Martin was flickering on the television screen. "She probably died of boredom." Had been Clive's quip to the genuine Doctor when he had come to certify the departure.

The only difference now was that the television was silent and of course, Auntie Sheila had long since gone to take her place beside the angels, or more probably if the vicar was to be believed, in a marginally lower realm.

"Poor Auntie Sheila." Marlene said as she walked into the lounge. "She always aspired to Sainsburys, but she could only afford the Co-op"

Clive had gone past sentimental. "We cleared all this out. How the hell can everything be back here? I remember burning that bloody thing when we cleared the place out." He pointed at a grubby knitted attempt at a sausage dog which Sheila had used as a draught excluder.

In the corner was a little brass hostess trolly with a gin bottle and a pair of tumblers. The original set was now in the corner of Marlene and Clive's dining room back in

Sedgewood. "That's just too bizarre."

"What's in the kitchen?" Clive pointed at the door.

Just like the hallway and lounge, everything was exactly as they remembered it. There were biscuits in the china biscuit barrel, the cupboards were full of tins and packets and there was food in the fridge.

Clive reached in and plucked out a half full milk bottle which he sniffed. "It's still fresh. Come to think of it, I could use a brew."

There, in the most surreal of circumstances, they made a pot of tea. Clive reached into one of the cupboards and picked up two mugs. Marlene looked at them for a second and then said. "You can't use that one, that's auntie Sheila's." Clive had obediently selected a different mug.

Some of the members of the congregation had also gone to visit the homes of their relatives as part of their travels too, and a far more cohesive picture was emerging.

As long as at least one person in the congregation had experienced something prior to the disappearance of all the other people, then everyone else now present, could also see, hear, or read it.

Where no one had been, such as the inside of Sedgewood or Bumfords Library, all that existed was an empty shell.

At some point during the night, all the shops the congregation had taken things from, magically replenished the missing items. Water, gas, and electricity all seemed to flow perfectly, and anyone could drive as far as they liked, and not need to refill with fuel.

The phones didn't work and neither did the internet. There

were no television programs although as Keith and Roger
had discovered before them, some DVDs and CDs could
be played.

The assorted pets of the congregation were all there, and a
few cats which people were used to seeing in certain places
according to their routine.

The world outside of Sedgewood appeared to reflect this
too. There were roads and miles of countryside, there were
buildings and pylons and telegraph poles. There just
weren't any people.

The discussions went on for some time and the
congregation kept looking to Marlene and Clive to explain
what was happening.

Silently, Clive , for the first time in his life, had been
praying.

Clive asked, and Caligula had answered.

"Tell them you're all in Elysium." He'd had to shout quite
loudly.

Marlene had been praying too. Caligula and Mata Hari had
obviously been discussing things as Marlene had been told
repeatedly that she was in 'a good place now.'

At just before midnight, Clive had clambered up the few
steps to the top of the pulpit and waved his hands to bring
silence to the room.

"Brothers and sisters, I have asked for guidance, and so too
has Marlene."

A sea of expectant faces looked up eagerly.

Clive continued.

" I don't know what has caused the transition, but we

believe we have all ascended."

For a brief moment, there was stunned silence, and then after what felt like an eternity, somebody at the back began slowly clapping.

As the applause slowly began to spread, Tim and James slipped away from the crowd.

"Fantastic!" James whooped once they were outside. "Free beer forever."

"Yeah, and clean pants too!" came the reply. "Let's go and celebrate!"

"But what about women?" asked Tim in a rare moment of forethought.

"Oh, someone's bound to give in eventually" answered James "After all, we're two of the richest and best-looking blokes in Sedgewood now."

It was Tuesday morning when the switchboard in Sedgewood's little police station came alive. Concerned relatives and employers inundated the beleaguered little team who spent hours logging calls, promising each caller they'd come and take a formal statement at the earliest opportunity.

This just wasn't reasonable. Mandy made everyone sausage baps on a Tuesday and by lunchtime, not a single sausage had been consumed.

It soon became apparent to Dan Rapier and his colleagues, that they were going to need assistance. By 10am, they'd had reports of at least sixteen people who hadn't been seen since Friday evening.
Noone had made the connection that the missing were all members of the same congregation.
The Sarge got on the phone to central.

The Sergeant, Robin Gittings, had already tasked Dan with looking into the strange incident with the missing taxi driver, and of course, the other incident.
Roger Parkinson, a constant source of call's and complaints, had been reported missing by the official neighbourhood watch group.
Normally, they diarised his peculiar activities and his bizarre behaviour was one of the most interesting things the group ever discussed or dealt with.
This included monitoring the little towns CCTV recordings. Roger was last seen entering a garden on Cedar Avenue in the small hours of the morning and had failed to

re-emerge at any-time after.

The houses on Cedar Avenue backed on to the school, and that was well covered with night vision cameras. There was no sign of Roger on any of them. It was as if he'd vanished into a portal.

Dan Rapier had driven to Norma's house to ask whether she knew anything of her strange brothers whereabouts. Norma it appeared, was having a party for one when Dan arrived. Bert Kemfert's 'A swinging safari' was playing loudly and Norma opened the door clutching a pint glass full of pink and yellow liquid, decorated with a paper umbrella and a chunk of pineapple. She was happy, welcoming, and quite clearly plastered.

'No,' she said, she hadn't seen Roger for several days. 'No,' she didn't know where he was. 'No,' she certainly didn't care. And finally, if they did find him safe and well, could they please lock him up and throw away the key?

Dan had left having learned nothing of any interest whatsoever.

Keith the Taxi lay face down on his mother's sofa, snoring quietly. His guide, Marc, had enjoyed the musicals at first, but he'd never much cared for alcohol, and he was getting a little bored with what had become the routine now.

Keith had consumed countless bottles of sherry and had then graduated to finishing his afternoons with pints of neat apricot brandy. He'd been oblivious to Marc's presence for most of his life, but now, the ingestion of so much spirit, was giving Keith the impression he could see spirits himself.

He could, there was a bottle of brandy and half a bottle of Mandarin Napoleon in mum's sideboard. What Keith thought he was seeing though, were just shadows from the telly and from the big lime tree just outside.

Marc could have sat on his lap, and he wouldn't have known. In fact when he'd run out of musicals and put on the T-Rex concert video, Marc had danced excitedly all over the room, and sung along to all of his hits. Still Keith hadn't twigged he was not alone.

While Keith slept, Marc had conjured a little red invisible mini, and gone for a spin around Sedgewood, being careful to avoid any trees.

There was Roger Parkinson, sneaking around as usual. Marc had checked the life plan for Keith he'd been given. Roger and Keith had a shared destiny, so it would be time to get them together soon.

Marc sent out a telepathic call, and in an instant, Norman

was sitting in the passenger seat beside him.

"Thanks for calling me Marc, it's an honour! I always loved your music."

Marc blushed a little and glanced at Norman. "Well to be honest Mr Wisdom, I'm the one who is honoured, I loved your films, The Early Bird is my absolute favourite."

"Please, please, call me Norman. Tell you what, can you pull over? It's just I get a bit carsick sometimes."

Marc gently came to a halt and parked neatly alongside the grass on the edge of Sedgewood's duck pond. Excited ducks scrambled to leave the water and head towards the little car. Just like the ducks in the original little town, the ducks knew that people, meant bread, or sometimes doughnuts. It didn't matter that the car and the two Spirit guides were invisible to all the humans, the ducks could see everything.

In fact, if the human population had ever realised just how perceptive and per-psychic the ducks were, they'd have been flabbergasted by what the feathered quackers knew. It's probably just as well that ducks can't talk.

On clambering out of the mini, Marc materialised a small bag of duck food and began offering it to the excited mass of waggling bills and bottoms.

Norman immediately fell over. It was an old habit. He put his hand up apologetically as he clambered to his feet.

"Sorry, sorry, just can't help Ooooooooooo" as, arms going windmill fashion, he tripped over a pushy Muscovy.

Norman clambered to his feet again and managed to stagger to a bench where Marc joined him.

"At least you can't fall off a bench, eh Norman?" Marc smiled.

"Wanna bet" answered Norman with a cheeky wink.

Roger and Keith were scheduled to meet in two days' time. Marc and Norman began planning exactly as to how this was going to happen. Arrangements made, Marc offered "Seeing as we're at opposite sides of town, I can give you a lift back if you like? As long as you're not carsick of course?"

"Yeah, okay then, thanks. I'll try not to fall over." Norman did his best , but he still tripped as he attempted to clamber into the passenger seat. Once they were underway, Norman looked to Marc and asked, "If you don't mind me asking, what's your one like?"

Marc gave a short laugh and answered "Well, to be honest, he's a bit of a weird one. I wouldn't choose him as a friend."

"Yeah, mine too." Norman answered, nodding thoughtfully.

Back in the original Sedgewood, Sam and Miranda were discussing recent events over a few glasses of wine with Dan Rapier. Nigel and Kevin were happily frolicking in the garden. It was a warm, sunny evening, and the effect of Miranda's wonderful lasagna and a few glasses of Chianti had been a soothing balm to their friends heightened stress level.

By now, you'd have had to have been in a coma not to have heard of the extraordinary disappearance of at least forty-two residents of the peaceful little town. The media had been covering the story for days and had interviewed just about anyone local they could corner.

As the residents of Sedgewood had been enjoying the Council Tossing celebrations, every single person known to have become an activist for Sedgewood's bizarre new religious order, had vanished. So too had the infamous Roger-neighbourhood-Watch-Parkinson, and Creepy Keith the Taxi. In most cases, the only people who appeared concerned, had been the mum's of the vanished, who according to Dan, were now in the process of forming their own pressure movement.

"Most of that lot would be lucky to get their bowels moving, let alone the government" Dan quipped as he explained what the Mum's had been up to. "If they think the Chief Constable is going to release any more officers, they're in la-la land.....which is where they were before all this got started anyway."

Miranda raised an eyebrow at Dan's unusual condescending remark. "Oh? Did you know some of the mum's then? Here, let me top that up for you" She leaned over the table and continued to ply Dan with Chianti. He took another mouthful and continued.

"Oh god yeah, we were at school with half a dozen of the missing fella's, weren't we Sam?"

Sam nodded. He and Miranda had already discussed this when the names of the missing had appeared in the Sedgewood gazette.

Dan continued. "You know that thing with the W.I in most places?"

He looked from Sam to Miranda and then back again waiting for a Yes.

"Hmmm? Jam and Jerusalem?" Miranda put in as required.

"Yeah that. Well they don't do that here" Dan grinned.

"Here it's more like Home-Brew, Steely Dan, and Jean Masons home-grown."

He glanced again from face to face and emptied his glass again.

Miranda couldn't conceal her surprise. "You mean dear old Jean from the pottery shop?"

"Yeah that's right. And I'll tell you what, yes, thanks I will have a top up, I don't know what strain she grows, but it's the nicest weed any of us at the station have ever tried!"

"Oh my god" Sam looked horrified, that's my auntie on Dad's side. Have you pulled her in then?"

"Oh yeah, I forgot that. Oh thanks Miranda love." Dan smiled at them both as he lifted his glass again. "Oh and erm, No. We haven't arrested her or anything. There's no point. We just got an anonymous note, in Roger Parkinsons handwriting, to go and check out her conservatory a few years back. Me and Robin Gittings went." Dan laughed "You wouldn't have believed how many plants she had in there, and the greenhouse, and all along the canal at the back too."

Sam was still trying to get used to the idea that Auntie Jean was growing cannabis. That was clearly why he wasn't ever allowed past the lounge, even though it had been Jean who had encouraged him to be a gardener in the first place.

"So what happened? How long ago?"

Oh ages, about seven, maybe eight years ago?"

Sam could hardly believe his ears. To him, this was bigger news than the 42-missing people.

Dan took another large gulp before continuing. "Cor, thanks you two, I had no idea how tense I'd been. Anyway! Getting back to Jean. The Sarge said to let her carry on. It was obvious a load of the, how shall we say, seniors, were smoking weed, we were getting reports of smoke smells from all over town. The sarge asked me to go plain clothes and just watch for a few days, and from what I could work out, no money was changing hands, it was like a community service type thing. Jean was giving out bags of weed to the older folk who were struggling with arthritis. Do you remember when they started having disco afternoons for the OAP's in Norris McWhirter Park? Well that was when."

Miranda was as surprised as Sam and sat wide eyed trying to picture the scene. Sam was unable to conceal his astonishment, his face was a picture. Auntie Jean. Dear little, cuddly, sweet, rosy cheeked Auntie Jean, stoned, bless her.

Dan carried on.

"It was really good for the town really." You could hear the approval in his voice. "The queues at the doctors vanished, the RTA's, bumps mostly, came to a complete stop as everyone was using the shuttle buses." Dan winked "Probably too stoned to drive. Oh and the other thing of course was that all the graffiti on the personal parking spaces of the councillors stopped. Everyone was happy. Well, now it looks like some of the older ones have been sharing the harvest, you know, with the would be Jam and Jerusalem's, so here we are, it's Steely Dan, Deep heat, and Jean's home-grown."

There were several minutes silence while Sam and Miranda let the revelation sink in. Finally Sam looked up and said, "And what was the bit about you and everyone at the station?"
"Oh well you see" Dan looked up "We always like to try a bit, just so we know what we're dealing with. Normally the Sarge makes us draw lots to see who the guineapig is going to be, you know, you got to find something in your work to laugh about. But anyway, this stuff was so nice we all tried it." He took another mouthful of the lubricating red and added "It's way, way better than that stuff you tried growing when we were kids Sam."

The conversation veered off into Sam and Dan's tales from their teens for a while, until Miranda skilfully brought them back to the topic of the missing residents. "I'm sorry Dan, I know you probably don't want to think about it, but all those missing people, what about their pets? I mean, some of them must have had cats and dogs, or other animals. I can't imagine that everyone has emergency plans in place like we do with Nigel and Kevin?"

Dan nodded. "Yes you're right, but one thing that we did find was that virtually all of the people who phoned in someone as being missing, did so because they were looking after somebody's cat or dog, or in Kieth the Taxi's case, his snake."

Miranda shuddered. "I don't think I want to think about Keith the Taxi's snake thanks."

"Sounds like he would have let you hold it if you'd wanted to." Sam chipped in with a cheeky twinkle.

"Oh stop it Sam, you're horrible." Miranda slapped his leg playfully.

Miranda finally saw the chance she'd been waiting for to ask the question she'd been pondering all evening.

"Does anyone have any idea what might have happened to everyone yet Dan?"

Dan Rapier had been asked that question more times than he could remember now.

"I can only tell you the same thing the spokesman told the press, we have no leads at all, just a mystery."

Miranda tilted her head to one side and slowly stroked her neck while locking Dan's eye's with her own intense stare. If Miranda had ever had to conduct SAS style interrogations, she'd have had the toughest men melting within minutes. Dan Rapier was no tougher and he succumbed easily.

"Just between the three of us, oh, and the whole of CID and MI5 of course, the thing is, we don't know how any of it links up, and nobody so far has any theories"

"MI5? Really" Sam took his turn, he was equally fascinated

to know what had happened, but with completely different reasons from Miranda.

"Yeah, we've had the whole lot, including some branches of government we're not even allowed to look at." He touched a finger to his lips "You know, 'Men in Black' types"

"Lummy" was all Sam could manage. He was feeling the effects of the Chianti himself; he rose to fetch another bottle. Nigel and Kevin both came bounding up to him, just in case he happened to be going anywhere close to the kitchen.

Miranda knew how to play the rest of her enquiries now; she'd been rehearsing while she'd been walking Nigel on the towpath. Funny that, she'd sometimes thought she could smell something herbal when she got close to auntie Jeans house. That was a different topic entirely though, Miranda needed information.

"Well now" she began "I've written on all sorts of topics, but I've never had to cover anything like this. This is real X-Files stuff. Has anyone got any theories Dan? Didn't that taxi driver vanish on the Monday? We all saw those" she paused momentarily, wondering whether or not to use the word she'd rehearsed "pillocks from the , whatever they called their nonsense church. They were here on the Friday, that's the day the ice cream van comes, I remember it."

"Yes we have some of that on CCTV, I've got to say Miranda, you don't hang about when the van shows up do you?" He laughed.

Miranda was caught completely off guard for a moment.

Dan quickly continued "Colin Parker over the road has about twenty different cameras set up, including half a dozen in the trees believe it or not. He says it's because he works shifts but we think he was keeping tabs on Roger Parkinsons movements."

Miranda's heart skipped a beat as her mind raced. What if Colins cameras had caught her sending Roger packing from her garden?

The sound of the fridge being rummaged through reached both their ears. In a minute, Sam would reappear bearing a predictable mountain of cheese and crackers and a selection of his home-made pickles.

"Why would anyone want to keep tabs on him?" Miranda was genuinely puzzled.

"Oh you'd be surprised Miranda. Roger Parkinson made loads of enemies with all his sneaking around, and worse. We had more than thirty people come forward with night vision recordings of him sneaking around all over the town…hang on Sam, let me help"

Dan got to his feet and took a heavily overladen tray from Sam and deftly relieved him of the bottle he had tucked under his arm too.

"Dig in, I'll get the rest."

Dan laughed again, they'd eaten a huge meal, but Sam, being active all day, knew a thing or two about burning off calories.

Dan waited until Sam had returned with even more food. Glasses were refilled and the chiminea lit.

Dan was supposed to be off work tomorrow, Miranda was

working from home again, and Sam had come to that blissful time in the season where all he had to do was keep a watchful eye on his poly-tunnels and greenhouses. It was going to be a late one.

At last everything was settled again, and Miranda could continue her enquiries. "Tell Sam what you were just telling me about Roger Parkinson" was her re-opening gambit. "Oh sure, yeah, where were we? Oh yes, Mr Parkinson. Well, it seems our Roger was creeping around just about anywhere and everywhere he could get into. There's masses of footage of him from over thirty cameras." This time it was Sams turn to be astonished again. "Thirty?" he muffled through a mouthful of Truffle Brie.
Dan nodded and reached for a lump of the Brie himself before continuing "Oo, that's lovely. Yeah, our Roger had seriously pissed off loads of people, and it gets worse. It'll be in the papers at the weekend anyway seeing as those journo's have been talking to so many people." He left a pause knowing full well that Miranda and Sam were dying to find out more about creepy Roger. Everyone in town was, except his sister.
"Well you see Mr Parkinson had keys for lots of places too."

"Noooooo" Sam and Miranda echoed in unison.
"Yes indeed! He used to hang around for long enough to see where people kept their spare keys, and while they were out, he used to get spares cut. Jimmy down at Right-Cut told us when he began to get suspicious. We could never prove anything then though, and it appears Roger had secret caches hidden away all over town too. We think in

the end, he began either cutting or making his own keys somehow."

"Crickey" was all Sam could manage, reaching for the Gouda now.

Dan carried on between mouthfuls. "Until they got wise to it, our Roger used to get keys off estate agents too.

Again, both Sam and Miranda chorused "Noooooo! How?"

"Oh he used to phone up and pretend to be the vendor, and say that he, Roger, had been booked in to clean the carpets, so he'd be along to borrow the key they had for viewings. We reckon he must have had at least a couple of hundred keys for different places.

"Noooooo!"

"Yes. Shocking isn't it. It would have made our job a hell of a lot easier if everyone who'd known something, had actually come forward and told us."

"So what do you personally think has happened Dan" This was the big one. Would Miranda be in any way implicated? She'd run the whole ridiculous scenario through her head more times than she could think. Every time, she would see the image of the Blocked button in her mind's eye.

Surely, she couldn't really have sent everyone away, could she?

The biggest problem for Miranda was, she still kept meeting irritating people, and she wanted them to vanish too.

"Oh I don't know" Dan was shaking his head. "I wouldn't be surprised if we find Mr Parkinson in a shallow grave having died suddenly from unnatural causes." He paused to swallow a glass of water Miranda had thoughtfully produced a little earlier.

"The rest of them though, I haven't got a ruddy clue. And neither has anybody else on the team. Look, we've been good friends and I wouldn't dream of saying this to anybody else on the planet, but when we did the background checks, we didn't find one single person among the vanished, who you couldn't have put on the weird and freaky list"

Sam was properly warming to this now. In the small town where he'd lived all his life, he knew at least half the people who'd vanished. He'd never had any of them pegged to be in the shifty brigade though. He wanted to know more. "Come on mate, we want to know everything. Spill the lot!"

"You pour, and I'll talk." Dan grinned at his old friend and held out his glass for a refill.

After what followed, Sam and Miranda would never view anybody in Sedgewood the same way ever again.

Later, as they got ready for bed, the conversation still focussed on the recently vanished inhabitants of Sedgewood. "I just can't get my head around Brian Corby doing nude decorating." Sam was shaking his head "I mean, doing your own place is fine, but fancy breaking into other people's places and giving the kitchen a revamp while they spend two happy weeks in Benidorm, in the buff? That's just plain weird that is!"

"Sam darling, I'm glad you feel that way. But hey, what about Linda Harper and all that peeing?"

Sam poked his head around the bathroom door to answer "Yeah, how bizarre is that. When you were up here having a wee, Dan said that they had her on camera pissing on gnomes in front gardens virtually everywhere from Clarence road right over to Elm Meadows. She was almost as prolific as Roger. What the fuck was all that about?" Linda Harper had been Dan and Sams form tutor at secondary school. Apparently she had something against lawn ornaments and had been filmed at all hours of the day expressing her feelings.

"You know the one that really got me though 'Rand?" Sam only ever called Miranda, Rand ,when he was full of wine and all loved up.

"Go on?" Miranda and Sam had both sat there in stunned silence as their dear friend had come out with revelation after revelation.

"It was that thing about Bernie Carter and those hamsters, I mean, what was he thinking, those poor little Beggers." Bernie was another of Sams cousins. He worked as a mechanic from a unit on the little industrial estate. He also had a second, secret unit. Bernie had become a member of the Church of the Eternally Confused almost as soon as it had sprung to life.

For his peculiarity, Bernie, like nude decorator Brian, had waited until people were away on holiday. In his secret unit, he was successfully breeding European Hamsters, great big ones.

For some reason, known only to himself, he would wait until a house was unoccupied and then through a letter box, or open window, he would, as Dan had so beautifully

put it, 'Gift' the owners as many hamsters as he happened
to be able to transport. In fairness, he would also pour in a
good helping of hamster food through whatever opening
he'd found...or sometimes made.

For years now, the population of Sedgewood had thought
they had a serious hamster problem.
There were suspicions of course. The trouble was, the
police had never actually managed to catch Bernie away
from his unit with a single hamster, so they couldn't prove
anything.
All the CCTV had confirmed what people were beginning
to suspect though, owing to Bernie's regular purchases of
vast quantities of hamster fodder.

In fact, the combined CCTV had revealed an incredibly
seedy underbelly that most of the town's residents were
completely oblivious to. Individually, an astonishing
number of residents had secrets.

Sam and Miranda settled down to sleep. No doubt Sam
would be snoring in no time and Miranda would be going
through to the other bedroom.
"I'll see you in a few minutes." she whispered to Nigel who
was currently at the bottom of the stairs, waiting.

In blocked World, Roger Parkinson was retracing his steps. It had all gone strange after that Boycott woman had let her horrible dog out to savage him. As Sam began to snore in earnest, in New Sedgewood, Roger began to explore Sam and Miranda's garden again.

He would have gone in the daytime, but Roger was becoming aware that there were a few other people here now too. He hadn't spoken with any of them yet, but from the few he'd observed, they looked like a right bunch of dysfunctionals.

Those two mummies boys for instance, Hammer and Tong, what he didn't know about those two wasn't worth knowing. Roger was talking to himself as he went.

"All their sneaking around? Perverts! That's what they are!" He'd seen them going into the Pickled Parson and helping themselves. "Disgusting!"

Norman, who was following Roger on his nocturnal perambulation, suddenly remembered that Roger had wanted to improve his diet by eating some real food.

"Sausages" he whispered in Rogers ear.

"Oh yeah, I must stop off at Joy's shop and pick up some sausages" he muttered to himself.

Norman nodded approvingly, he was getting the hang of this Spirit guide malarkey now "Good lad" he said, and promptly tripped over a hedgehog. "Oha" he giggled "Who put that there?"

Sam's guide in the meantime, had decided it was time for a few hours off. He decided to go and have a look around. Dave loved to know what was going on. Like Norman, when he'd been in human form, Dave had loved to hear people laughing, he brought a lot of his humour with him from his physical life to his role as Sams principle guide. There were a few times he thought he might have overdone it a bit with some of his suggestions to Sam and his naughty sense of humour. So far though, the boss had just smiled and let him carry on.

Dave loved to observe, and because of this, he was as aware of what was going on in New Sedgewood as he was in Sam and Miranda's source world.

At the moment for instance, That Parkinson fellow was about to come into the garden, and who was that with him? Dave thought himself to the front gate to intercept the visitors. Of course, only Norman could see him.

Norman was still trying to get to his feet, having fallen over twice more in the process. No matter how he tried, his knees just seemed to go in separate directions, a bit like him and Roger right now. He felt Dave materialise.

"Who's that then?" Asked Norman in a voice only the other Spirit guides could hear.

Dave stepped forward and extended his hand. "Hello old friend, fancy seeing you here. You know, your name was on the life plan all along and I never realised it was you."

Norman was delighted and lit up like a firework display. "Oo, Oo, I can't believe it, fancy seeing you here Dave. This is wonderful. He reached out his hand and promptly tripped into Daves arms. "Oh bless you. Well isn't this a turnup for the books, me old mate, Dave Allen."

"It's just Dave now Norman. Hey, looks like you landed a right one there?" Dave jerked a thumb towards Roger.

"Yeah, I know, but it's my first time, and that chap Peter said the committee always gives everyone a numpty to start with. Do you fancy a cuppa?"

"Well, I wouldn't mind a drop of whisky, there's some inside. Thankfully, my chap likes the good stuff" Dave answered with a smile and a wink. "He'll be okay for half an hour" he gestured Roger again. "Let's go in shall we?" Dave indicated the door of Miranda and Sam's New Sedgewood house.

Neither of the Spirit guides heard the growling coming from inside from Blocked World Nigel. The minute the door was opened, he came rushing out into the garden barking frantically.

"Oh bloody hell!" the two Spirit guides heard Roger cry out in desperation. Mr Parkinson was obviously in his own world now, which was a world of panic, and he flew past them in a desperate attempt to exit the garden while Nigel pursued him barking for all his spaniel worth.

"Shouldn't I be helping him?" Norman looked at Dave.

"Well the thing is Norman, that's a part of the job too. We have to let them learn their life lessons don't we?"

Norman nodded "Yeah, well, I suppose so"

"And anyway" Dave gestured towards the source of the diminishing noise as Roger made it to the end of the road with Nigel in hot pursuit "Nigel's having a lovely time. He's never had a chance to chase Roger like that before, and I wouldn't want to spoil his fun."

Norman thought about this for a moment and answered, "Yes of course. Thanks Dave, this is all still quite new to me. I know that you've been hopping timelines, but I wasn't ready for all that at first. I wasn't sure whether I could do this Spirit guide thing."

"I'll pop the kettle on. Do have a seat." Dave gestured towards the table where in Source World, Sam and Miranda usually sat.

Norman tuned into Roger for a second and informed his old friend. "I think they're almost down by the post office now. I never realised that Roger could run so far."

"I bet he didn't either" Dave answered as he came back into the kitchen clutching a bottle of superior Irish whiskey "You see, Norman? Every cloud eh? It's a good experience for him."

They laughed for a moment and then Norman said, "Anyway Dave, got any new jokes?"

"As it happens, I've got a great one about when the seven dwarves went to the Vatican" Dave answered with a twinkle in his eye.

"Fantastic!" Norman answered and added, "Oh, and you'll never guess who I'm working with at the moment." And then added "Tra-la-la-la-la-la-la."

Dan Rapier awoke to the sensation of something warm, bristly, and wet, licking his neck. He was face down on his mattress. He'd managed to get his shoes and his shirt off when he'd arrived home, but he still had his jeans on, and his bladder was threatening to burst. The additional weight of Kevin lying on his back and enthusiastically slurping sweat off his human didn't much help his situation either.

Dan tried to look at the world through eyes that were so bloodshot, he was fearful of opening them properly in case he began bleeding to death. His head was pounding like a jackhammer, and he didn't even have the energy to feel sorry for himself.

"Oh come on Kev, mate, get off me will you?"

Reluctantly, Kevin clambered off. The amiable spaniel followed his human through to the bathroom where Dan lifted the lid and plonked himself down to release the pressure in his bladder. Standing up at a point like this would have required far too much energy.

He'd probably said far too much last night, but he trusted Miranda and Sam, and anyway, as he'd said, the papers would be full of stories about Sedgewood and the forty-two missing residents.

Everyone was hoping there wouldn't be any more strange disappearances, well at least that's what they were saying in public.

Secretly, most of the population had a little list in their heads of people who they wouldn't mind disappearing altogether. In a candid moment, Sargeant Robin Gittings had confided in Dan "It's like wanker bingo, but with people."

Dan had laughed as his old friend and mentor had continued mockingly "Oo goody, that's another one gone. Brilliant, HOUSE! I wonder who the winner is?"

Neither Dan nor Robin knew, but the winner of course, was Miranda.

It was Saturday. The only reason Dan was off today was the huge number of hours he'd put in over the previous week. It had been frenetic in work. The police station just wasn't big enough, and so initially, to the delight of the pupils at Sedgewood's two primary schools, classes had ceased, and the expanded police force had moved in.

Having two locations so far apart had proven impractical, and so after the second day, the senior pupils of the secondary school had been relocated to their former places of incarceration.

Like the primary school pupils, the lower years were given an early summer holiday.

During this period, very little actual police work had been conducted, however, excited members of the public, as he'd told his friends last night, had begun bringing in their thousands of hours of digitised CCTV footage.

It was going to be a monumental task to make sense of it all.

In the meantime, he'd asked Joy in the newsagents to drop him off a copy of every single local and national newspaper she could get this weekend. Perhaps they'd already arrived? Dan didn't know what time it was, but it was light, the birds were singing, and he'd heard a motorbike a few seconds ago, so obviously the world was awake and moving around.

 He left the bathroom and headed down the stairs, followed enthusiastically by Kevin. No newspapers had arrived yet he noticed. He shuffled into the kitchen and glanced at the clock; it was just after 5am. "Oh bloody hell Kev, just once, you could have given me a lie in." The spaniel grinned at him as Dan began searching through the kitchen drawers to find some appropriate painkillers.

The next three hours were a cocktail of misery ranging from extreme pain to knee weakening nausea. How much Chianti had he drunk for goodness sake?
Miranda knew, she'd drip fed him at least three bottles to loosen his tongue. Nicely of course. She could have saved herself at least two bottles, he'd have told them everything anyway.
Dan was brought back into reality by an abrupt clattering on the door. It was Joy herself.
"Blimmin heck, you look like you've just been exhumed" were her warm words of greeting as he opened the door.
"That bad huh? To be honest Joy, I feel like I have too. How come you're here? Everything okay?"
"Oh yeah, sure, well, I'm doing way better than you are anyway" She grinned knowingly. "Bit of a late one was it?"
"Hmm, yeah, old friends" Dan managed to mumble, he was feeling nauseous again. There was nothing for it, he

knew the only way to sort this one was going to be a Bloody Mary.

Joy was one of the biggest gossips in Sedgewood, but she also had a good streak of kindness running through her and Dan knew it.

"Look, I had to bring the van, it's those papers you wanted. There's no way Thomas could have carried that lot." She waved her hand in the general direction of the road. She'd left the car in the middle of the narrow street, in such a position that cars coming in both directions were having to mount the kerbs to get past. Joy was oblivious. "Can you give me a hand?" and then "If you're up to it that is?"

Twenty minutes later, Dan was curled up on the floor in amongst the biggest pile of newspapers he'd ever purchased. He'd given Joy a fifty-pound note with a request that she come back quickly with a bottle of vodka and some more painkillers. Luckily, he already had tomato juice.

No doubt Dan Rapier and his tragic drink and drug issues, to wit, one solitary hangover, would be the talk of the shop today. By lunchtime he'd have probably been labelled as Sedgewood's very own Oliver Reed or Keith Richards. Dan didn't care, Dan was in the grips of purgatory, it was a price worth paying.

Joy, bless her heart, had even offered to take Kevin for a walk around the common, after she'd dropped off the vodka, Dan had made her promise. In the meantime, Kevin was enjoying a ride around his hometown in the little newsagents Rascal.

Despite his discomfort, Dan began scanning the headlines.
THE SEDGEWOOD TRIANGLE one headline
proclaimed. BRITAINS STRANGEST TOWN, AND IT'S
MISSING PECULIAR INHABITANTS announced
another. WHERE ARE THEY NOW? asked another. Dan
continued to work his way through the articles, hoping to
garner as much information as he could from the
somewhat unguarded statements some of the still present
residents had made about the absentees. It had to be said,
there wasn't a great deal of flattering going on so far. One
article mentioned the missing taxi driver and included a
statement from Linda, the coordinator of the taxis. She was
quoted as having said, "To be honest, everybody always
thought he was a bit of a sleaze, even his friends don't
really like him that much, but I hope he's okay."
Several of the articles mentioned Clive and Marlene and
speculated as to what might have happened. Had they, as
some residents had suggested, taken all the money, and
gone to live on an island in the Maldives?

One of the papers had the words APPEAL across the front
page. The newspaper owners had helpfully made available
an information hotline that the public could call.
Apparently, it was to help with the ongoing enquiries. Dan
went on to read the small print and learned that you could
call this line for just seven pounds a minute.
No doubt Sedgewood's already stretched police presence
would be inundated with calls about that too once irate
residents began to discover they'd been scammed.

The Grindlebury Times, predictably Dan thought, barely

gave this huge event a mention. Their coverage this week was mainly about a local radio and television celebrity who'd been caught shoplifting, yet again.

And lastly, having read through dozens of articles and headlines now, Dan came to the paper he loathed the most, the Daily Hate. HUNDREDS MISSING FROM SMALL ENGLISH TOWN, PROBABLY MURDERED. WAS IT THE IMMIGRANTS THAT DID IT? Dan managed to muster the energy to take that one straight outside and dump it on top of his barbecue. He popped back inside momentarily to pick up a cigarette lighter and then set fire to it.

"Vile piece of filth" he exclaimed as he watched the flames consume the hateful rhetoric.

Joy arrived with the vodka. "I'm happy to have Kevin for a few hours, you look like you could use a sleep love."

Joy was correct, Dan had been working ceaselessly since Roger and Kieth had vanished. Since the reports of the missing members of the congregation of the Church of the Eternally Confused had been coming in, he'd barely slept at all.

After Joy had gone, Dan forced himself to drink a single large 'medicinal' Bloody Mary and went straight back to bed.

As he closed his eyes, unfelt by him, Dan's Spirit guide leaned over, brushed his hair back and kissed him gently on the forehead.

"You rest now Dan" She'd said gently.

She was known simply as Bee these days. Her full name

was a bit of a mouthful.

It had been Bee's idea to suggest a Bloody Mary. It had also been Bee's idea to suggest, through Joy's own Spirit guide, that Joy have a day's fun with happy spaniel, Kevin.

Of all the Spirit guides, Bee was the only one who'd read the entire life plans of everyone who was presently, and about to become entangled with Blocked World, at least where Dan was concerned.

Something truly tragic was about to occur, and she needed Dan to be strong enough to get through it.

In both Source World, and New Sedgewood, there were the first signs that the long, light summer days were beginning to shorten. The sycamores reached vigorously for the sky in a bid to grow as much as they possibly could until autumn arrested their development. Apples, plums, and pears began to swell in the orchards. Sams courgettes and French beans were growing almost as quickly as he could pick them. Nothing was wasted, anything Sam's customers couldn't consume, was either turned into chutney and then sold around the town or gifted to the little animal sanctuary on the northern side of Sedgewood. Apparently Porcupines and Capybara loved courgettes.

In source world, despite microscopic examination of all the CCTV footage and thousands of man hours consumed with enquiries, still not one shred of useful evidence had come to light about the whereabouts of the missing residents. The most plausible theory anyone could come up with was a mass alien abduction. Media speculation remained intense, nothing like this had ever happened before, anywhere.

In Joy's shop, the conversation had been about little else. It was the same in the pubs and at the Friday Market. Miranda in particular was interested to learn whether anyone had discovered anything new. Sam, being Sam, had shied away from the speculation and subsequent gossip, and had focussed instead on his magnificent potatoes and strawberries.

The gossip flowed as unstoppable as the wind, aided by the

daily statements made by the police spokesman to the eagerly waiting press.

There was also now another distinct group who wanted to know what the latest developments were. Like vultures, some of the distant and estranged family members of the missing, had begun making enquiries into what they might stand to inherit. Dan Rapier had found signposting some of those people to their own solicitors truly distasteful.

From an investigative point of view, Dan was getting to know each of the missing individuals far better than he'd ever wanted to.
Now, as Dan was beginning to find out, it was astonishing just how many of them had police cautions or criminal convictions, many acquired during periods of residence away from the little market town.

The Sargeant, being the senior man present, had known of some things, but there was very little to alert Sedgewood police to most of the darker elements of the current population. So few incidents in the town itself had ever been reported, and very few people knew that Sedgewood's little community was anything but an ideal of perfect behaviour.
They couldn't have been more wrong.

A search of the homes of the missing had turned up an equally unsettling array of 'personal items' and 'Items of questionable origin' as the squad were describing them. Dan had come to the conclusion that, without exception, there wasn't one person among the missing, that he would actually be relieved to see back in the community.

Freaks, Weirdos, Oddbods, Perverts, Con-artists, Stalkers, Embezzlers, Thieves, Bullies, Vandals, Thugs, they were all represented. The squad had run out of adjectives to describe them. In fact, one or two of the more experienced officers were beginning to say in private "Never had a group of people deserved to be disappeared so much" and that "Whoever had done this, had done a huge service to the community"

It was no wonder that they'd all gone searching for salvation at the Church of the Eternally Confused.

It was a harsh judgement, but one which those with access to all the available information were increasingly in agreement with.

Miranda would have been relieved. Miranda was the only person in Sedgewood who had a genuine theory about what had happened. What troubled her most was, where were they all now?

Wherever it was, she hadn't wanted anybody to suffer, well, except Roger perhaps.

In the small hours of the morning, she'd pondered the question, what happens to people if you block them on social media? Well, she reasoned, they carried on their lives, but without being able to see the presence of the person who blocked them.

That was fine with Miranda, perhaps they were all just carrying on their lives in an alternative reality then?

Freya and Nostradamus had laughed uncontrollably when

Miranda had unknowingly reached that conclusion.
In fact, Mirandas intuitive knowledge of the quantum universe was far greater than Miranda had ever realised. Now she just needed to realise that she knew what she knew.

Miranda also had a second notion which she found equally troubling. What would happen if any of those dreadful people ever managed to find their way back to her reality? She did her best to compartmentalise that thought and bury it beneath happier ones. Assuming that anyone who she'd blocked was still safe and well, and if it really had been Miranda who had sent them away, perhaps they'd like some company? There were certainly a few people still in Sedgewood whose presence she and Sam wouldn't miss. Miranda fluctuated between warming to this idea, and feeling guilty that she was responsible, not for the disappearances, but for all the frustrations of those who were investigating.

In all other ways, life in Sedgewood, and the rest of the world carried on.

In New Sedgewood, the original members of the Church of the Eternally Confused had disbanded. What was the point of attending services if they'd already ascended? By the time things began to get fractious, Clive and Marlene hadn't been seen for a week.

A few members of the former congregation who were still speaking to one another, had speculated that perhaps the founders had gone to Rhyl? Those who'd known Marlene before the ascension, knew that she'd always had her heart set on a little bungalow in the seaside town.

In truth, Clive and Marlene had hidden themselves away in the Vicarage. Nobody would look for them there. They needed to come to terms with the new world they found themselves in. They also needed to come up with some way of remaining the authority figures before their former followers decided to turn on them and exact their own form of retribution. Luckily, the vicar and his wife had been well stocked with both food and alcohol. Clive had discovered that the vicars taste in porn had been identical to his own and was spending his evenings in the cellar, flicking through the well-thumbed pages of the vicars collection of *Dirty habits* magazines. Clive was beginning to suspect that the ladies in the photographs might not be real nuns after all.

Upstairs, Marlene was busy watching old video recordings of reality television shows while guzzling cocktails and consuming a seemingly endless supply of anchovies on sesame and poppy seed crackers. There was also a full set of Fred Dibnah videos, and although she'd seen them before, she was looking forward to going through the entire collection again.

A handful of the congregation had been seen heading off in vehicles loaded with personal possessions and heading in different directions away from the little town. None of these vehicles or their passengers had been seen since.

In New Sedgewood, things were becoming anarchic. People were becoming territorial and were claiming rows of houses, or in one case, an entire street. Some of the buildings had been burned to the ground, such as the secondary school and the council offices. The next day though, the buildings had rematerialized and looked as if nothing at all had happened.

The Hammer and Tong lads had torched the school for a second time, and a third, and had eventually given up as every time they tried to destroy something, it would magically reappear, completely intact, the next day. Between drinking bouts in the Pickled Parson, they never tired of smashing the supermarket windows though.

A trio of the relocated, had decided to have a go at driving as they'd never got around to having lessons in their former lives. It seemed sensible now they could go anywhere they wanted. Margery Proctor and Valarie Thompson were having lessons with their beleaguered husbands. Progress was slow, and the crash of impacts with both stationary items and the few other moving vehicles, was a kind of soundtrack to the otherwise peaceful days. Luckily so far, no one had been seriously injured although Mr Proctor and Mr Thompson had almost come to blows over who was allowed to drive on the ring road at specific times of day. Billy Baker had never learned to drive either. Too arrogant to ask for anybody's help, Billy had decided that he was going to learn in the towns fire engine. It took him two days to get the sliding doors of the fire station open. When he had managed to launch the beast into the street, he'd immediately crashed across the road, demolishing the war memorial, and finally finishing wedged in the front window of the police station.

This had all miraculously repaired itself by the following morning, whereupon Billy repeated the performance, but this time managed to include a hitherto undamaged police van.

Day three of this particular time loop was when Roger, still undiscovered by the former church members, had decided to move to new dwellings.

Roger Parkinson was muttering to himself as usual. It was approaching 4am and he was in the process of moving his newly acquired, mostly camo and tactical belongings. He would have gone back to his sister's house, "my ruddy 'ouse anyway" he chuntered as he thought about it again briefly. What had put him off that idea was the thought that Miranda Boycotts dog lived over on that side of Sedgewood. "Bloody thing." He muttered for the hundredth time.

Norman and Marc were watching. Norman was curious.

"How come spaniel Nigel is here and at the same time, he's in the Source World? I don't get it?"

Marc had been Spirit Guiding for a while now and had crossed the time barrier to visit different centuries too. Marc knew enough about how things worked that he could have written a new album if he'd felt the urge.

Since the last time he and Norman had met, Marc had received a rare memo from the boss, asking him to help Norman ease into his new role.

The Guides were supposed to have left Ego behind when they'd departed their earth-bound bodies. Most of the guides hadn't quite accomplished that, and Marc's Ego was still as present as it had ever been. He'd been delighted to be recognised, and he considered his new additional duties as equally important as his original brief.

He smiled at Norman and thought both of them into the place of NO-TIME. As the two stood in the centre of a mass of stella bodies, Marc explained "Well you see Norman, it's all down to the function of Quantum Superposition."

"Oh." Was all Norman could manage, he was more than a little out of his depth, and trying to stand upright in space when there was no obvious horizon, was one of his greatest challenges ever. He did his best.

Marc continued. "Well what happens is down to a function of the quantum field you see?"

Norman nodded despite still being none the wiser. "It's what Einstein called spooky action at a distance, or perhaps that was quantum entanglement? I'll tell you what, he can explain it better"

In an instant, who should appear floating in space beside them but the legendary physicist himself. "Sorry for the delay" Albert extended his hand in greeting "I was busy on that Facebook thing, trying to take away all the quotes which people say are from me, but aren't. Those Fact checkers are useless, and they're full of sh..." He stopped himself just in time, took a breath and continued

"In fact I'm still there mostly, while I'm here talking to you" Albert laughed and winked at Marc "You see? There it goes again. It's pretty useful this superposition lark!" Norman, although it would have seemed even more impossible, looked even more confused.

"Oh that's no problem sir" Marc answered, "It only felt like there was a relatively short delay from where we're standing." Albert gave a polite little laugh, but Marc could tell the genius before him had probably heard that particular attempted joke so many times that repeating the same action and expecting different results was probably insanity.

"I was hoping you might be able to explain to Norman all about quantum superposition Mr Einstein sir?" Marc asked, but in a far less flippant tone now.

Albert was happy, he was going to discuss his favourite subject.

"You see, there are many strands and timelines running through the multiverse, and they're all connected, you see?" Marc nodded; Norman was busy being Norman and was doing his best not to fall over again. There was far too much 'You see-ing' going on.

Albert carried on anyway.

"When we, my team I mean, and other physicists, when we began to look at the tiny particles which make up our multiverse, we learned that sometimes, in fact many times, a single particle can appear in two places in the same instant of beingness, what human beings call time. You see?"

Normans head was beginning to hurt. Albert continued.

"And we also found that sometimes a particle was visible, and sometimes it disappeared completely, as if it vanished from existence, a bit like Mr Schrodinger and his famous cat."

Norman was wishing he'd never asked.

"So you see" Albert continued, while gesturing at the cosmos in general "sometimes, the same thing can appear in two places at once and be entirely whole and complete. It's not two particles, it's one, just one."

Norman was really struggling now. He looked confused, and a little scared.

Albert was in full flow now though, and Normans expression did nothing to deter him. He continued to deliver statements bullet fashion in his heavily accented English.

"Sometimes it vanishes from sight while it hops between timelines and realities. That is what has happened to the people in Blocked World." He paused for effect
" But Nigel and the other animals, they exist in both places simultaneously, living different but equal lives. You understand now?"

Norman didn't understand at all. He felt as if he were back

at school. He wished his old school physics teacher were here. Mr Oswald had a way of explaining things that Norman had understood.

"I have to go now" and with that, Albert vanished.

The boss had clearly been looking in, as in Alberts place, with the briefest of sparkly twinkles, Mr Oswald appeared. Norman was a little taken aback. The last time he'd seen Mr Oswald, he'd looked as if he were about one hundred years old and he'd been wearing a tweed suit, and a university gown and mitre. Here he was dressed in some rather close-fitting lycra leggings, a brightly coloured open necked shirt and very little else. His blond hair had been shaped into a…was that supposed to be a daffodil? He looked as if he was about 20 years old. There was no mistaking it though, it was definitely him.

"Hello Norman, great to see you after all this time, I followed your films you know? You did really well. Good lad! I always knew you were never going to be a scientist." He smiled warmly and noticed Normans now even more bewildered expression "Oh this? Do excuse me, I was at a Kylie concert in Barcelona. Isn't she fantastic?" Marc agreed, Norman was still speechless. Mr Oswald took the cue. "I understand you need some clarification on quantum super position, well now Norman, it's like this…"

If the clock had been running in the NO-TIME, it would have been several days before Norman and Marc emerged back in Blocked World.

"Yeah, I get it now" Norman was nodding enthusiastically

as the rest of the universe resumed its machinations. He and Marc returned their attention to Roger "I really get it, thanks Marc, you're a pal!"

Roger was huffing and puffing. "One-more-load." He panted as he put the last of his stolen ration packs into the wheelbarrow he'd acquired from the allotments.

Roger was heading towards Sedgewood's telephone exchange. He'd been working on his new home for a week. First he'd had to break in. Then the bloody window had repaired itself, and he'd had to break in again. On day three he'd remembered that Tall Nick, the telephone engineer, had lived in a house just behind the police station. Roger had been there before on his 'night patrols' and he definitely remembered seeing several bunches of keys hanging up on the kitchen wall, next to the breadbin. Roger had almost cried for joy when, on searching the kitchen, he'd found Nicks spare set of master keys for the exchange.

Roger went back inside the police station for one last time and glanced around to check whether he'd missed anything. Satisfied that everything he considered important was now either on the wheelbarrow, or already at the telephone exchange, he began the last arduous trip across the town.

Roger had carefully planned his route to avoid all of the residences of the congregation. Most of them would be asleep, but around a quarter of them, he'd been surprised to learn, also enjoyed a nocturnal foray out into the deserted streets. He'd almost reached the end of Fairfield Road when he had to abandon the barrow, and dive into Mrs Winstanley's hydrangea, in order to avoid bumping into Shuan Bu'Mole.

Norman cast a short-lasting cloak of invisibility over

Rogers protruding boots.

Shaun, Roger had learned from his stealthy observations, was a voyeur. He didn't just like to watch in real time, he also set up tiny cameras to record people through their bedroom windows, or if he could gain entry, from inside. Roger quietly admired Shaun, but right now wasn't the time to begin a conversation. At the moment, nobody from the church knew that Roger was there, and Roger wanted things to remain that way. "Silly old bat." He muttered after Shaun, seemingly oblivious to the wheelbarrow, had gone past "Somebody should have told her to trim her ruddy bush. Look at it poking out everywhere."
As it happened, Shaun had spotted the wheelbarrow loaded up with an assortment of items, but in Sedgewood now, as the inhabitants settled into their new lives and set about acquiring everything and anything they liked the look of, there were wheelbarrows and random piles of belongings dotted all over the town.

Shaun was in a hurry; he'd just collected the SD card from the camera he'd left in Julie Fowlers bathroom. If only she'd known, Julie was another member of the congregation. Currently, she was blissfully unaware of Shaun's perversions, but quite fancied Shaun Bu'Mole anyway, and she had a few perversions of her own.

Roger picked a few hydrangea twigs from his hair and clothing, and taking up the wheelbarrow, continued on his way.
Norman looked on. "Not long now." He told himself.

Earlier in the day, for the first time in weeks, Marc had finally managed to get through properly to Kieth. Marc had had to go into the screen of the T-Rex live at Wembley video. "Put down the alcohol" he kept telling Kieth from the screen. As though hypnotised, at last, Kieth had complied. Marc was hugely relieved; he had been working on this for days.

Kieth had fallen asleep again and so Marc had whispered a set of instructions directly into his ears until he was certain the message had been received.

When Kieth awoke, he blearily began following the instructions.

Firstly, he had to go back to his own flat. The clock on the wall had told him it was 4am, the stars were visible and the moon shone brightly.

Kieth felt horribly hung over. He went to his mum's little bathroom and began rummaging around in her prescription stash in the bathroom stool to see what he could find.

As he left his mums little bungalow for the first time in almost a month, the thing that stood out to Kieth the most, was the eerie absence of traffic noises. Even at 4am, there were generally still a few vehicles moving around. The posties were on their way to work and a lone police car would drive endless boring circuits on a route so regular and predictable, it had become pointless. Anyone with long journeys to make would be clambering into their cars too, along with the packers at the egg farm and those early morning or late-night workers who lived their lives while others lay dreaming.

Feeling uncomfortable and exposed, he did his best to hurry. The quickest way back to his own place was along Elm Tree road, through the playing fields, and then along the back of the supermarket carpark and onto Redlands Parade. He navigated all of this without seeing, or hearing, a single person. As far as Keith knew, he was still the only one here.

The last short section was the stretch across Fairfield Road, and onto Barbican View, where his flat was, above the now deathly silent fish and chip shop.

Kieth had been a little unsteady on his legs at first, but Marc had kept whispering to him to spur him on.

"Nearly there now" Kieth congratulated himself as he turned the corner into Fairfield, and in a stunt Norman would have been proud of, tripped spectacularly over the wheelbarrow, the contents, and even more surprisingly for both of them, over Roger Parkinson.

They hit the ground with a thump that made the lime tree quiver. The shock of discovering one another proved even greater than the shock of the impact.

They managed to untangle themselves, and both crawled, and then pulled themselves up into a somewhat slouched postural echo, facing one another, and trying to come up with something to say.

"Say hello" Marc whispered in Kieth's ear.

"Roger!, well fuck me! I never thought I'd be pleased to see you." Kieth blurted out, and then, before Roger could answer "Who else is here? I mean is everybody here? I mean, is everything normal? I think something really fucking strange happened to me."

Roger considered Kieth for a minute. In the past, the taxi driver, the one all the women called creepy Kieth, had been pleasant enough to Roger, unlike a great many of the other residents of Sedgewood.

As far as Roger was concerned, they were stuck here, and, as far as he could tell, that lot from that church were a right bunch of assholes.

It would probably be a good idea to have someone on his side anyway, wouldn't it?

Roger didn't know it, but just as Marc had been programming Keith, Norman had been subliminally programming Roger.

"Golly! It's Kieth isn't it? I don't know what to say…. Erm, no, everybody isn't here as it happens, but there's a few of us, not that I've spoken to anybody yet. You'd better come with me."

Kieth thought about this for a second as the disappointment slowly filtered through.

What was this place? He vaguely remembered something called Purgatory, which was on the way to the afterlife wasn't it? This must be it. "Oh god" he groaned. Despite having swallowed a generous quantity of mother's medication, his hangover seemed to reach a new level of misery.

"I have to go home." He told Roger "I have to feed Kellog and have a shower." As the words left his mouth, Kieth realised he'd been wearing the same pair of underpants since things had first turned peculiar. "…..and change my clothes" he reached up with both hands to clutch his temples, "…and get some painkillers"

"Hmmm, okay then." Naturally, Roger already knew where Kieth lived and that it wasn't far. "Let me tuck this away a moment." He gestured at the spilled contents of the wheelbarrow.

As the darkness of night began to give way to the pale grey of dawn, and the first of the early birds began their busy day, under Rogers guidance, the strange duo made their way quietly toward Kieth's flat.

Marc and Norman congratulated one another, the life plans had said that Roger and Kieth had been scheduled to meet. In their last lives, They had been arch enemies who'd hated the sight of one another. In this life, the life plans said, they were destined to work cooperatively together.

"Let's leave them to it for a bit shall we? I don't usually drink alcohol, but I'm happy to sit and watch you have a pint or two if you like Norman?"

"I think that's a blimmin good idea" Norman answered,, and then said with a chuckle "Did you see how he flew over that wheelbarrow? That was magnificent. Couldn't 'ave done a better job myself!

Would you mind if I invited my old mate Dave? He's a right laugh."

Sam had a mystery on his hands and he was upset. Somebody was stealing fruit from his allotment under cover of darkness.

He'd gone to do some watering at 6am one morning. The sky was bright with promise. There was hardly anyone around, and he'd cycled from home with Nigel happily running just ahead of him. Past the back of the school they went, along the old canal path, "oh yes, well fancy that!" There was no mistaking the herbal smell as he rode past auntie Jean's house. Along by the back of the telephone exchange and then down the old pack horse track to the open fields and patchwork quilt of allotments and poly tunnels.

The first thing he noticed as he propped the bike up against his shed, was that the door of his middle tunnel was open. Sam never left the tunnels open at night. Sometimes the deer would get in, and the deer, he'd learnt to his cost, loved melons and they loved tomatoes.
"Oh bloody hell Nigel, what do you thinks happened here?"
Nigel woofed in answer and followed his master as he hurried towards the open polythene door. Inside, to Sam's huge relief, there didn't appear to be any obvious damage at first. When he reached the middle of the tunnel though, where he'd been nurturing half a dozen melon vines, without a doubt, someone had removed the four largest melons from their carefully constructed hammocks.
The vines were torn and there were small footprints in the compost beds.

"Bloody hell! Who on earth would do a thing like that?"
Nigel looked up at his human sympathetically. Sam shook
his head in disbelief. Anyone who knew Sam Boycott
would have known he'd have happily given away his
produce to anyone who might have been struggling
financially, so this was a real blow to Sam. Why on earth
would anybody need to steel from him?

He checked the rest of the tunnel and then went into the
other tunnels to hastily check them over too. Fortunately,
there at least, his cucumbers and aubergines were
untouched.

The fruit garden was a different story. The door to the fruit
cage was gaping open, and the poor strawberry plants
looked as if a heard of elephants had passed through.
The beautiful little primitivo vines he'd been so lovingly
nurturing had been plundered too, damaging the plants
severely in the process. Big strips of bark had been torn off
with the bunches of grapes. "Who? Why?" Sam would
never be able to understand the thinking of the sort of
people who did this. Miranda called them entitled. Sam
called them vandals and thieves.

Sam did what he could to tie up and bind the broken vines,
and finally at just before 9am, went to his shed to slump
down and wallow in his despair.

The strawberry plants were wrecked, the melon vines had
sustained so much bruising they would probably collapse,
and if they survived at all, the grapes would take months to
recover too.

Nigel did his best to comfort his human, he could see poor
Sam was upset.

Half an hour had passed with Nigel resting his chin gently in Sams lap. The alert spaniel picked up his ears and gave a gentle 'woof' as the sound of an engine could be heard approaching.

Sam roused himself from his dismay, it was Paul Tanner who worked the tunnels next to his own.

Sam rose to his feet and stepped outside of his shed to raise a hand to his neighbour.

"Alright Sam. Beautiful morning eh?" Paul called out cheerfully as he clambered down from his Land Rover

"Hi Paul" Paul could tell at once that Sam wasn't his usual self. Nigel looked as if he'd lost his bounce too. "I'd better tell you what's happened" Sam continued "I haven't checked yours at all mate. Sorry. I wasn't thinking"

"Oh hell, are you okay mate?" Sam wasn't.

"How about we check yours first and then I'll show you over here?" Sam gestured the tunnels and began walking towards the path that ran from the watering station he'd built, to the tunnels where Paul grew catnip and wasabi and a few unusual peppers commercially.

As they checked Pauls patch, Sam explained what he'd discovered on his arrival. They were both relieved to see that Pauls crops appeared unmolested.

They went to view Sam's patch next, and learned that whoever the thief was, they had also taken the crop of Wine Cap mushrooms he'd so patiently cultivated. Sam was livid. Paul was angry too.

"If you call the police Sam, I'll get my CCTV from last night."

"CCTV?" This was big news to Sam "I had no idea you

had such a thing. I haven't seen any cameras."

Paul gestured towards his shed. "Oh it's easy these days, the cameras are tiny, they run on batteries, and they work over the wi-fi. Two tics and I'll get the memory card and adaptor."

A few minutes later, Paul had returned clutching a memory card and a device not much larger than a credit card. As Sam put the kettle on in his little refuge, Paul plugged a wire into his phone and began fast forwarding through the previous night's recording. "It only goes off when it catches a movement" he explained. The camera angle was directly down the path to the main gate. "It doesn't cover our tunnels Sam, but if anyone came up that path, they'll be on here" Paul continued.

The allotment was surprisingly busy at night. The camera had activated for a handful of pheasants, a family of badgers who'd passed through, several rabbits, a hedgehog, a young couple who'd been holding hands, out for a romantic stroll, and a single inquisitive fox. "Golly, I never realised it got this busy" Sam said as he took a sip of his tea. "Oh, look, what's that?"

On the small screen, Sam and Paul watched a large, light-coloured vehicle pull up. Two people got out, women by the looks of things. First one, then the other clambered over the gate. There followed a flurry of activity where the two women made several trips up and down the path as they loaded their stolen produce into the truck. On the very last trip, one of the women looked up for long enough for Sam to be able to see her face clearly. It was Kristen, that horrible toxic woman from Berkeley Buildings.

From the way she moved, Sam was pretty certain he knew who the other one was too.

The smaller woman clambered back over the gate, and as the vehicle manoeuvred to turn, just for an instant, the numberplate was visible. TOYA1.

"I'm calling the police right now" Sam said firmly.

"They won't do anything unless you can identify those two." Paul countered in a slightly disappointed voice.

"Oh that's just fine mate. I know exactly who those two are, and I know exactly where they live."

"I'll help you with the watering then until the law get here." Paul offered. They often helped one another out.

Dan Rapier was delighted when the call from the allotments came in from control. Anything to get away from the dead-end investigation and the thousands of pointless, but sometimes disturbing leads that the squad was receiving. Only this morning, MI6 had supplied a file which revealed that Milinda and Brian Gates had a history of abducting and drugging the drivers of ice cream vans and cake lorries, and then stealing their loads. They were wanted all over the country. The more the squad dug, the more genuinely bizarre the congregation had shown its members to be.

By lunchtime, Dan had taken a statement from both Sam and Paul, and then used the patrol car to go and fetch all three of them some bacon baps. Tea and sunshine was a far more pleasant way to spend the morning. Dan recognised the number plate too.

"You must let us deal with this Sam." He'd told his friend earnestly. "You mustn't approach them or speak to them. In fact, do me a favour buddy? Don't go anywhere near Berkeley until we've had a chance to haul them in will you?"

Sam nodded slowly in agreement. "I'll tell you what Sam, you know I'm not supposed to do this, but I'll send you a text once I've seen them." Dan took another bite from his bap. "I'll see you later anyway, you're having Kevin tonight aren't you?"
Sam remembered, oh yes, Kevin the spaniel was coming to stay. Dan Rapier had summoned the courage to ask one of the visiting police officers out on a date.
"Yeah, sure thing mate. Nigel's looking forward to it, aren't you Nige?" he rubbed his four-legged friends head. Nigel woofed approvingly.

Reluctantly, Dan rose from his chair and began to walk slowly back to the police car. "I'll see you later mate, and like I said, stay away?"

Later, when Sam had done his best to rescue the battered plants, he thanked Paul for all his help, and clambered back on the bicycle to cycle home.

Later, when Miranda asked him why he'd come by that particular route, he'd struggled to explain why exactly he'd ignored their friend, and cycled back along the pack horse track, up the tow path, and then turned straight onto Highfield Avenue, the only road which on his way back to his house, would take him right past Berkeley Buildings.

Sam had been upset by the thefts at the allotments, but what he saw now felt like a punch in the stomach.
His beautiful Laburnum tree was gone. All that remained was a brutalised stump and a pile of chainsaw debris.

When Miranda came home, she found Sams bicycle left where he'd dropped it on the driveway.
Nigel was sitting underneath the kitchen table, pressed up against Sams legs, doing his best to console his human.
Miranda was shocked, Sam was sobbing his heart out.

It was late now; Sam was breathing deeply as he lay beside Miranda. Earlier, between his sobs, Miranda had learned all about the incident at the allotment, and then the callous felling of the beautiful yellow blossomed sentinel, which Sam had nurtured, fed, and watered.

Dan Rapier had come by to drop Kevin off and had confirmed that Both Kristen and Toya would be having an overnight stay at the police station. The CCTV had clearly shown their guilt, but the subsequent visit to Berkeley Buildings had sealed their fate. Dan had recalled his afternoon.

Dan had spoken to his sergeant who had jumped at the chance to get away from the Missing persons incident rooms for an hour . Having viewed the footage again, the pair embarked on the short journey to Berkeley Buildings. They chatted in the car on the way there.

"That Kristen woman. Is she the one they call wolf eyes?" Dan knew exactly what Robin was getting at.
"It is. She's not been here long and she's getting a terrible name for using people."
Robin nodded in acknowledgement. "From what I've been hearing, she's not averse to helping herself to things either" he glanced over at Dan. Robin continued, "It'll be interesting to have a proper look around that place. Sam Boycott made it really nice didn't he? It used to be one of the roughest dives in town."
"Yeah, he did. He worked on that like a Trojan; I don't think it looked that good for all my life."

Dan knew this was true, when he and Sam had been children, they'd built dens in the overgrown garden.

"What happened to that beautiful tree?" the sergeant had asked Dan as they'd pulled into the driveway "I dunno sarge. Sam's going to be gutted, that was his memorial for his dad."
Robin Gittings frowned, he and Sam's father had been close friends. He'd watched Sam grow up, and as one of the many people who'd spoken at the funeral, he'd given a beautiful eulogy.
He knew exactly how much that tree would have meant to Sam.

First they'd looked through the windows of Toya's monster truck. There were wine-cap mushrooms and grapes scattered on the back seat.
Dan remained collected and professional; Robin Gittings was quietly fuming.

Kristen hadn't answered her doorbell, and so Dan and his sergeant had gone through the little gate which led to Toya's porch. The door was open, and there in clear view on the kitchen table, was a big pile of grapes, melons, strawberries, and wine-caps.
Kristen was sitting on one side of the table and Toya was on the other. There was a half full wine bottle between them, and three empty ones. There was also a brick sized, leafy block of something that both looked and smelt as if it might be illegal, sitting on a chopping block beside the sink.
Both Dan and Robin's experienced eyes had estimated it

probably weighed at least a kilo.

When Robin Gittings rapped loudly on the doorframe, both women raised several inches from their seats. Kristen had been mid-sentence "….and he said he'd give me guitar lessons and I intend to get my money's worth. Oo! Golly you made us jump."
She began hastily attempting to stub out the Jaz woodbine she'd been holding.

The women had blanched, and from their panicked expressions, both of them knew that they'd been caught red handed. Despite this Toya, when asked directly "Where did all the fresh produce come from?" had attempted to lie and tell the visiting police officers that she'd just come back from Waitrose.
"And what exactly is that? Ornamental Jamaican stinging nettles?" The sergeant had pointed at the worktop. Handcuffs had been produced, colleagues had been summoned, and back at the police station, the two women had been unceremoniously shoved into cells at oposit ends of a long corridor.
"We'll just let them sweat until the morning shall we?" had been the sergeants word. "At least we know now who's bringing that contaminated, nasty spiked weed into town. Bloody spice. I didn't use to worry when it was pure herbs." he'd told Dan.

Sam had barely nodded as his friend had filled him in with the details. Kevin, normally so full of springer springiness, had gone to join Nigel under the table. Now both spaniels were trying to console Sam.

Dan had left, and for the remainder of the evening, Sam had barely spoken.

Miranda could feel Sam's pain. The melons, the mushrooms, and grapes, he could have dealt with that. The beautiful tree though, that had been a deliberately spiteful act, and a completely unnecessary one. Why was it that some people were just such horrible assholes? Miranda asked the ether.

In her mind's eye, she could see the smug faces of Nosferatu and her sidekick Toya. Miranda began to focus on the pair and brought the image of the big red BLOCKED button into her vision. As a last-minute thought, she added in Nosferatu's boyfriend, Renfield. He was a dishonest, useless bag of shit too Miranda decided. And then with a firm push, she mentally depressed the button.

In Sedgewood's police station, there was a brief sucking noise, followed by a plop. Where there had been two cells with occupants, there was now nobody.

Renfield had been on the other side of Sedgewood. Some evenings, he gave guitar lessons to his friends son, or so he said to Kristen. In reality, he'd been on the sofa at his ex-girlfriend's house and was just putting his underpants back on. Debbie had gone to the toilet. When she came out, his jeans and tee-shirt were there, but her part time lover had gone.

Clive and Marlenes attempt to hide in the Vicarage had been discovered. They knew they were in hot water now. They'd been able to sustain the fantasy that everyone had gone to heaven for a little while, but then, inevitably, the awkward questions had begun again.

"How come my knees still hurt?"
"I thought I'd be young again?"
"I was certain my auntie Vera was going to be here, actually, how come it's just us?"
"How come it still rains?"
"Why can't I fly like Superman?"
Even though most of the congregation had now dispersed around New Sedgewood, the demand for answers kept coming.

Clive and Marlene had offered to spend half an hour each day at the mostly redundant meeting hall where they would do their best to answer any queries. It was tedious, but they were properly down the hole now, and they just couldn't stop digging.

Caligula and Mata Hari were both fed up too. They were doing their best to answer Clive and Marlenes calls for help.
They would telepathically suggest things which the pair of con-artists then thought were their own ideas.
It was becoming terribly complicated now though, and what they needed was some advice from some of the greatest liars of all time.
They'd been flitting between dimensions listening to British Politicians and tabloid journalists seeking ideas and

inspiration.

Even with all the additional help, what happened next really let the cat out of the bag.

Despite being able to do whatever they liked, Louise and Rita still managed to find things to complain about. They complained about everyone else, and then, like true sisters of the eternal victimhood, they turned on one another. They'd have come to blows if several of the other inhabitants of new Sedgewood hadn't intervened. Clive and Marlene, along with some of the other congregation members, had begun to dread seeing the pair. No matter how good the day had been, they always managed to find something to whinge about.

Some of the congregation members avoided them like the plague, but not all. There was a distinct contingent who treated the whining women as entertainment. Even if they didn't have questions themselves, they would come to the church just to watch the show. It was the closest thing they had to reality TV and Soaps.

This morning, the pair had arrived before everyone else. they were right at the front of the church in floods of tears. The first few arrivals sniggered, but then began to realise that today, there might actually be something genuinely wrong.

Some of the parishioners attempted to discover the problem, but all they got in return was incoherent moaning. It was a huge relief to everyone when at last, Marlene and Clive arrived. Caligula and Mata Hari were late. Back in source world, they'd been enjoying a Conservative Party

Fantasy session, where the speaker had been announcing what their policies for the next year were to be.

In the House of the Church of the Eternally Confused, Clive had resorted to Holy Vodka to settle the girls down. Finally, between sobs, the story came out.

The girls had been up early. They'd been walking to Joy's shop to stock up on cream eggs and flakes before anyone else could get there, when unusually for that time of day, they'd heard whispering.

They'd hurriedly secreted themselves behind some bushes in one of the gardens and peered out between the leaves to see who exactly was approaching.

"It was that horrible Roger Parkinson" Louise had managed to blurt out between gasping sobs.

The entire congregation did a Mexican gasp of surprise.

"And that creepy Kieth was with him" Rita managed to add in a bid not to lose her audience.

"And then" Louise wanted the attention for herself.

"That little twerp, that pub singer came prancing down the road like a frightened gazelle…."

"In just his pants" Rita shouted.

Clive and Marlene flinched. Now they knew that without a doubt, the game was up.

There was an awkward silence, and then someone at the front said slowly. "I thought you said that this was heaven?"

Another voice, from the back this time, quickly followed up with

"And that we were the only ones here?"

Looking on, Sam's guide Dave chuckled, he used to tell a joke like that.

It was a Mexican sniff now, and then a sob, until as one collective body, the entire assembled mass, including Clive and Marlene, had broken down in floods of tears and dismay.
Some of the other parishioners had arrived now. The quiet streets had been even quieter than normal, so they'd come looking to find out what had transpired. Somebody had rung the bell to summon the last few absent members.

By the time Caligula and Mata Hari reappeared, there was uproar.
Some people were upset, some were angry, and almost everyone was confused, except Tim and James. They just looked at each other, shrugged their shoulders, and went back to the pub.

Keith had heard the bell too. "I don't know what's going on, but I suppose we'd better go and find out?" Roger was hesitant, but even he'd grown tired of all the sneaking around. Reluctantly, he agreed.

In the police station, Kristen and Toya had heard it too, just as they were discovering that their cell doors were unlocked, and that there didn't seem to be anyone else in the building.
They made their way out into the eerily quiet little town, and then decided to head towards the ringing themselves. Kristen's boyfriend was heading towards the ringing too.

The last few hours had been strange beyond words. Perhaps he should write a song about it?

On their way to the Pickled Parson, James and Tim saw first Roger and Keith, then around the corner, Kristen, and Toya. Last of all, and now dressed in some of his own clothes again, was a very puzzled looking pub singer.
"Hey lads, what's going on?" he panted as he paused to catch his breath.
James jerked his thumb in the general direction of the ringing.
"Think you'd better get yourself down there mate, you'll find out all about it then."
"Yeah mate, I think they're probably expecting you."
The singer looked bewildered but did as suggested anyway.
"Yeah. Right. Okay. See-you." And then he took off again towards the slow tolling of the bell.
Tim grinned at his mate. "Do you reckon we ought to go back? I reckon it's gonna right kick off in a minute." And then for some bizarre reason that only they understood, the two began laughing hysterically.

Summer melted into autumn, and as the days began to shorten noticeably, Sam began to gather in his biggest annual harvest.

Potatoes were carefully lifted and stored in paper sacks. Onions were tied into strings and hung to dry. The little kitchen became a place of pickling and juicing and bottling as Sam kept himself occupied preserving fruit and vegetables in every way he could.

Miranda had been busy learning how to evade interrogation techniques on you-tube.

As one of the most well-known writers in the district, she had been appearing on television and radio shows to speak about her up-coming book release.

The interviewers always managed to slip in a few questions about Sedgewood's missing people.

The disappearance of the two women from Sedgewood's police station was the greatest mystery of all.

Much to Mirandas amusement, nobody had even noticed that Renfield was gone too.

Miranda kept her answers vague and speculative.

Only the most skilled of observers would have ever realised that Miranda knew a lot more than she was letting on.

Dan Rapier and the investigation team were still making startling discoveries about the nefarious backgrounds of the people who'd vanished. The more they looked, the less they actually wanted to find most of them.

In Sedgewood, life continued but the mood of the town was different. It was as if a huge shockwave had blasted out into the world, and almost everyone in town was on their best behaviour.

Under normal circumstances, the vacuum which nature abhorred, would have been equally rapidly refilled by another group of miscreants. In the case of Sedgewood, it was as if a magical ring of protection had been thrown around the town, and those with malintent, made sure they stayed as far from the town as humanly possible.

Almost everyone, but not quite.

Halloween was approaching. For years Sam had refused to grow pumpkins. He hated the fact that the perfectly edible pulp was so frequently just scraped out and hefted into the rubbish.

Then one year, his friend Rebecca who worked at the local animal park ,had put out a request on Radio-Mellow for all things pumpkin.

The unwanted pulp and seeds, and later the carved rinds, could all be used and preserved in a multitude of ways. The zebras and squirrel monkeys were delighted.

Sam had looked at squash growing through new eyes, and consequently, had occupied himself during the middle of October, with the harvesting and distribution of the orange giants.

He'd had a particularly busy day and was still out in his van when his phone rang. It was Miranda.

"Hi love, I'm in the Wizard's with Elaine, do you want to come and join us?" Sam could hear the strands of Werewolves of London playing in the background. Elaine was one of Mirandas best friends. He thought about it for a minute and then replied.

"I think I'll just let you two get on with it tonight. I'm guessing you could probably do with a catch up anyway? Is our boy with you?"

"I thought you'd probably say that, but it would have been rude not to ask. Yes, he's here, or at least he was….oh, he's chatting Tim up for some scratchings" Miranda laughed.

"Righto lovely. I still have a couple of drops to do. Do you want me to pick you up in a bit?"

"Oh, we're fine thanks. Tom is picking Elaine up so I'll grab a lift with them."

"Righto lovely, have fun, I love you."

"I love you too." And she was gone again.

Sam returned his thoughts to shifting pumpkins. They were great to grow, but oh boy, they took some shifting.

In the Wizards Staff, the bar was gradually filling up with tea-time customers. The fire was lit and the bar smelt comfortingly of woodsmoke. There was a bubble of conversation, and as usual, the atmosphere was convivial. Miranda tucked her phone back inside her bag, thanked the barman, and picked up two recently replenished wine glasses before making her way back to the table where Elaine was waiting for her.

The log fire crackled happily as the flames performed their unique ballet, sending orange and lilac dancers and the occasional cluster of sparks upwards into the medieval granite fireplace.

Miranda and Elaine exchanged news and gossip and to Miranda's relief, stayed right off the topic of all the absentees.

They'd been chatting for almost an hour when a tall, smartly dressed man approached their table, clearly intending to interrupt them.

"Good evening ladies. It's lovely here by the fire, do you mind if I join you?"

The table could have comfortably seated six people, and glancing around, Miranda could see that by now, most of the other chairs were taken. The decision was taken out of her hands when Elaine said, "Yes of course, have a seat." The man reached out to place a heavy mug of dark liquid on one of the beer mats before pulling out the chair opposite Miranda and taking a seat.

As he sat, Miranda had a flash of recognition, but she couldn't quite place him.

"I'm Andrew Morton he announced, offering his hand first to Miranda who took it hesitantly as she spoke her own name, and then to Elaine.

He gave them both a broad smile. To Miranda's acute senses, it was clear from his body language and eye movements that his attention was mostly on her.

Luckily, Elaine, beautiful, friendly gregarious Elaine, took the lead. Elaine should have been on the investigation team; she was an expert at extracting information about people.

"I don't think we've met before have we?" she asked before taking another sip from her glass.

"Oh I'm quite certain I'd have remembered the names of such beautiful ladies if we had" came the reply. He lifted his glass and took a few gulps of the frothy contents which prevented him from noticing Miranda as she performed one of her audible eye rolls.

"Hmm, well that's an interesting brew!" he declared, setting the glass firmly down again.

Elaine gave Miranda a sideways look. Elaine was a writer too, but she specialised mostly in screenplays. Sometimes, the two friends would collaborate on a magazine article. Their last piece had been for a ladies weekly and had been titled "How to avoid the pub Real Ale bore"

Both women began grinning. Miranda quickly covered it up by saying "Oh that's far too strong for me, I think I'll stick to the vino" she tapped her glass with her finger affirmatively and then took up where Elaine had left off "So what brings you to Sedgewood then Alan?" She was gratified to see him flinch involuntarily as she deliberately named him incorrectly. She lifted her glass to her lips as he answered.

"It's Andrew" he corrected her with a thin smile "I'm going to be taking over the veterinary practice in the new year."

In a searing flash, Miranda remembered the incident on her wedding anniversary.

The Andrew before her was the same Trevor Cooper lookalike she'd jabbed in the eye.

"Who was that idiot?" Miranda had asked as she and Sam had strolled along the riverbank afterwards.

"I'm not entirely sure, but I think he might be the new vet. He's taking over from Mr Wilson in a couple of months."

Sams voice seemed to echo as she mis-swallowed and then just as rapidly, coughed a slug of wine straight back into her glass.

There then ensued a coughing fit which almost brought the entire pub to a standstill as Miranda sputtered wine and phlegm into her scarf which thankfully, had been draped over the back of her chair.

Andrew, unhelpfully, decided to capitalise on the opportunity, and stood to move around to Mirandas side of the table, presumably to help her in some way. Elaine promptly pulled out her own chair and made sure she obstructed him.

The coughing eventually subsided and Miranda stood up, still clutching her scarf to her mouth, and indicated the general direction of the ladies toilet as she set off purposefully.

"I'd better go with her" Elaine offered in conciliatory tones and hurried after her friend.

In the privacy of the ladies lavatory, Miranda was waiting for her by the sinks.

"Are you okay now? Do you want me to call Tom?"

Miranda cleared her throat and answered "Oh god no. We have to stay. I want to know a bit more about Mister Andrew out there."

"Really? Alan?" Elaine laughed; she knew Miranda far too well to have assumed the name change was anything other than deliberate.

Miranda quickly reminded Elaine about her previous encounter with the new vet, finishing with "…Well! He deserved it!"

Elaine remembered the first time Miranda had recalled the tale, and she was on the scent now too.

"Okay then, let's find out a little more about our new mister Vet, did you want to toy with him for a bit?"

"Oh god no. Nothing like that, but I'm happy to do a bit of data mining"

"Alright then" Elaine agreed, "Let's get to work!"

They made their way back through the crowded bar where Miranda had to nod and say "Yes thanks, fine now" to a dozen concerned enquiries.

Back at the table by the fire, Andrew-vet-Trevor as Miranda was now mentally calling him, had finished his drink.

He rose to get a refill and asked, "Can I get either of you a refill?" Miranda had coughed phlegm into her glass and Elaine had knocked her own over in the kafuffle. Tim the landlord was just on his way over to clean up with a damp cloth having only just been released from serving.

"That would be lovely, thank you" Miranda answered for both of them. "Elaine always has the blush and I think I'd better switch to white. Tim knows which one, thanks."

The table was cleaned, glasses cleared away, and Andrew came back with the fresh offerings.

"Oh thanks Adam, that's really kind" Miranda gave him her warmest insincere smile. A frown flickered across his brow, but this time he didn't correct her.

There was something about this woman he thought, something familiar, but he just couldn't place her. The roller-decks in his memory circuits span around like Ferris wheels trying to locate that vital pinch of knowledge.

What followed was a subtle but thorough interrogation the most skilled of secret services would have been proud of. Andrew tried asking questions too, but he was so far out of his depth with Miranda and Elaine that the total information exchange went around ninety-five percent in their favour.

Miranda decided to visit the bar and ply him with a little more tongue loosener. Returning with a fresh pint for him she asked, "Sorry Adrian, you were telling us about your divorce?"

So far he'd been addressed as Alan, Adam, Arthur, Aiden, and Armand. He still hadn't realised he was being played with and had given up his attempts at correction.

Just as he was about to answer, Elaines phone bleeped.

Tom was outside, waiting.

"I'm so sorry Anthony, my husband's here to collect us. We really have to go. It's been lovely chatting with you." Andrew rose to his feet and offered his hand while making one last futile effort. "And it's lovely to meet you too. Oh, and it's Andrew?" He turned to say goodnight to Miranda too.

"It's been so lovely to meet you both. I'll send you that friends request on Social media."

Miranda and Elaine both mumbled something about how lovely that would be, politely said goodnight, and then headed to the door and their lift home.

"Well now, what do you think of that?" asked Elaine, turning to her friend in the back seat.

"Well actually, I don't think he's quite the berk I thought he was when we first met anyway…oh dear, I'm glad he didn't recognise me."

"How about coffee in the morning?" Elaine suggested. "If you accept his friend request, we can stalk his profile?"

"That's a great idea!" Miranda agreed.

In New Sedgewood, now that winter was approaching, the displaced residents were finding things to argue about. It should have been Utopia. Anything which was consumed from the food and drink outlets automatically replenished. Refuse vanished if it were left in a bin, and even the filthiest of garments would reappear laundered within a day if previously placed in a laundry basket. There was no cost for anything, the fruit and vegetables still appeared to follow the seasons, and there was plenty of countryside to expand into, but for some strange reason, nobody seemed to want to.

Some things changed. There had been signs of geese migrating overhead. The weather and day length was definitely changing, and after the first few weeks, items which had been damaged, such as the crashed vehicles, stopped repairing themselves and retained all the dents and buckles.

Meetings had been taking place; without Clive and Marlene. After the initial meeting on their arrival, Kristen and Toya had explained from their point of view, the events in the Sedgewood they'd come from, and the reactions of the remaining residents since the first disappearances. Renfield hadn't been allowed to speak. None of the trio had been able to work out how they'd been transferred. Adaptable to any situation she thought she could profit from, Kristens greedy little eyes were too busy finding potentials everywhere she looked. Perhaps she could become Queen here?

Toya had most been relieved to learn that her monster

Arctic Explorer was here, and her secret weed stash which she'd rapidly begun exchanging for favours. She seemed untroubled by the changes, for the time being anyway.

Clive and Marlene had been summoned to the town hall to explain themselves. Nobody wanted to go to the meeting hall since the discovery that they weren't all in heaven after all.

At 11am, the residents began shuffling into the big hallway which had been selected for what was expected to be an uncomfortable half hour.
Each resident was going to be allowed to express their grievances either about Clive and Marlene, or about any other resident if they thought they had cause.

Virtually everyone had something to say, and the complaints included absolutely everyone, even Toya and Kristen who had already begun pissing people off. Renfield wasn't popular either. He hadn't been well liked in Sedgewood in the first place. He'd soon found a PA and guitar in his new home, and his attempts at describing in song the forlorn situation he now found himself in, had been torturous to anyone with the misfortune to have been in earshot.

With no choice now other than to tell the entire truth going right back to the conception of the church, Clive, and Marlene, between angry shouts and threats of severe personal harm, had been forced to do exactly that.
At this point, Caligula and Mata Hari had reappeared.

Telling the truth was a huge development for both of their charges.

"Perhaps there's hope after all?" Caligula had suggested as they looked on.

The congregation was furious with Clive and Marlene, and then in the true spirit of the occasion, the accusations against all the other members of the congregation, and everyone else, had begun.

Roger Parkinson had attended, expecting to enjoy the show voyeuristically, but it wasn't long before he became a target himself. Kieth made a pathetically weak attempt to help Roger, albeit from a misplaced sense of obligation.

"Well I think it's a good job Roger has been so vigilant in keeping an eye on everything." He suggested foolishly. Clive, who had been the main target of the animosity up to that moment, seized the opportunity and shouted like a true bully "He always did sneak around a lot! We all know he's dodgy! Tosser!"

There was a collective intake of breath and a chilling, momentary silence before the assembled crowd turned their anger on Clive again and the shouting progressed to an outright melee.

As the heated, chaotic bickering and accusatory shouting escalated, the distinct ethereal figures of Marc Bolam and Norman Wisdom materialised beside Caligula and Mata Hari. Mata Hari greeted them warmly.

"Oh Hi you two. We were wondering where you were."

Marc gestured to a little marbled balcony set in the wall at first floor height up above the enquiry desk.

"We were just up there, but we thought it might be a bit safer if we came down, didn't we Norman?"

Caligula and Mata Hari nodded knowingly. Norman just smiled. "I can trip over just about anything you know?" He said with obvious pride.

The shouting was getting louder and more heated now.

"How come they can have the Vicarage?"

"That sodding idiot and all those garden gnomes….."

"…music was going until 4 am….."

"…greedy cow keeps taking all the crunchies…."

"….I just want the pool to myself for an hour occasionally…"

"….parks that bloody three-wheeler wherever he bloody well likes…"

With each accusation, a name was attached.

Things were going to get really nasty in a minute, Norman could tell, he'd just spotted a fleet of Spirit guide St Johns Ambulance volunteers turn up through the open doors.

Marc looked from Guide to Guide and explained, "I've been looking through the entire brief again, I suppose this was inevitable if you put together such a group of…" he paused, searching for the right word, "Dysfunctionals?"

"I'd have said 'dislikeable' too" Norman chipped in uncharacteristically.

Caligula and Mata Hari agreed without a speck of hesitation.

Marc continued "I think this is going to go on for a while.

Hey! I didn't used to drink while I was alive, but Normans been teaching me. Anyone fancy a pint?" He gestured towards the big oak double doors.

"What a splendid idea!" Caligula, always up for a slurp, beamed back at him and offered his arm to Mata Hari.

The foursome were leaving as the Hammer and Tong boys were arriving, each clutching a carrier bag full of something: just as the first fistfight broke out.

"Oh great, we're just in time." James told his friend. "There's nothing I love more than watching a group of complete idiots slog it out. Let's go round the side Tim, we can get up to the balcony then."

"Perfect!"

"I'm glad we remembered to bring beer!"

The boys guides , Judy Garland and Kenneth Williams quickly decided that they'd join Norman and company in the Wizards Staff. There was nothing they could do to get through to James and Timothy at the best of times. They'd both decided many years before just to sit this one out quietly on the sidelines and create their own entertainment.

Sam had gone to the market leaving a puzzled Nigel with Miranda at home. The bewildered spaniel didn't know yet that Dan Rapier was going to take both Nigel and his brother out to Doggyopolis. He'd gone to curl up in his own bed, which was unusual, but it was obvious to Miranda that Nigel was feeling a little hurt. He'd soon cheer up again once Dan arrived with Kevin.

Originally the park had been conceived to be part of a bigger caravan park, and was intended for people, not dogs. The planning, as a result of well-greased financial wheels, a few expensive dinners and a handful of complimentary holidays for the four main councillors; had gone through almost immediately. The construction had begun before the first lots on the proposed caravan park had even been pegged out.

This had backfired on the developers of the intended caravan park. The construction of the water slide had aroused a surge interest in the hitherto unpublicised development. The residents of Sedgewood were horrified at the idea of a caravan park right here beside their own little oasis, which was ironic considering the types of almost identical parks a good proportion of them stayed at themselves during their holidays.

A flurry of objections had swiftly halted any further progression, and after a short but impassioned battle, the corporation had decided to take their investors' money elsewhere.

The adventure park had stood completed, but subsequently unused, and unloved. That was until a few of the locals learnt that their dogs enjoyed swimming in the green algae which now filled the paddling pools and fountains.

A local couple had bought the site for a pittance and had quickly transformed a slowly crumbling eyesore into an asset for the entire community.

The green areas had become a sensory garden full of herbs which locals were welcome to pick for culinary use at home.

The pools and waterslide had been repaired and repainted and then filled with sparkling fresh water.

Behold! Doggyopolis had arrived.

Anyone could pay to use the amenities, but dogs and owners had priority during certain hours.

It all worked beautifully.

The only slight bone of contention on site was the big plantation of catnip which was being nurtured for resale commercially. More than half the cats in Sedgewood had been to investigate the delicious aroma. On the plus side, whenever a cat did go astray for a day or two, it was almost inevitable that they'd turn up safely at the park.

This had a knock-on effect as some of the visiting dogs had done their best to investigate the visiting cats. There had been several bopped noses and overall, the cats held the position of dominance.

Dan Rapier had taken the boys at the beginning of the summer, and they'd had a wonderful time. There was a doggy assault course, a 'chase-the-stuffed-rabbit' track, pools to splash around in, and even a selection of gourmet doggy treats. Nigel and Kevin especially liked the water slide.

Miranda sat in her office working on her latest piece. Elaine was scheduled to arrive at ten and then at midday, Dan was scheduled to collect Nigel. The boys would have the whole afternoon together. If Miranda could persuade Dan to bring Nigel back after tea-time, she might even mange to squeeze in an afternoon nap. The thought filled her with a warm glow. Miranda enjoyed napping just as much as Nigel did.

Miranda's phone bleeped. Apparently she'd received a friend request from an Andrew Morton, then she remembered the introduction from the night before. "Ohhhh, him. Hmmmm" She put her phone back on the desk beside the keyboard. "Not yet Mister Morton. Elaine and I are going to have a really good look at you before I give you access to my profile."

It was a lesson Miranda had learnt well. At times she'd joked that she must have some sort of invisible neon sign over her head which said, 'Weirdo's latch on here.'

In New Sedgewood, the disgruntled residents had begun to move houses again. The brawl which had gone on for almost twenty minutes, had shattered any remaining pretence of teamwork and cooperation, not that there had been a great deal of that anyway.

Initially, the congregation had been glued together in their desperate search for something meaningful. They had mostly suspended the more nefarious aspects of their behaviour while belonging to the church, but that restriction didn't apply any more.

A few small alliances had been born in the aftermath of the town hall punch up, but the overall feeling was an 'Everyone for themselves' approach.

Kristen and Toya had always operated like that and hadn't noticed any difference.

Renfield had written a song about the incident.

Roger Parkinson had introduced Taxi Keith to a whole new world. Roger didn't sneak around all night now; he'd found the CCTV hub for New Sedgewood in the Police Station when he'd made his residence there. He and Keith spent hours spying on the small group of Blocked World residents who had assumed that as there were no police, no one at all was watching.

Roger took great delight in giving an almost constant commentary in which he criticised virtually every action he witnessed.

His imagination and ego had made Roger an 'Important Person' before the changes, now he'd elevated himself to an almost godlike status.

Keith, having few other people to talk to, had actually begun warming to Roger. It was a subconscious survival mechanism, so he couldn't help himself.

Keith had his own agenda now. He was using the CCTV to track the movements of several of the ladies. If he learned their routines and how they liked to pass the time, he could use that to ooze up to them. Keith currently had designs on Kristen, Toya, Marlene Puddle and Rita Daub. His prime focus though was Louise Wattle. 'So what if she had a moustache and drank cans of Special Brew for breakfast' he thought to himself, 'She'd probably be grateful for the attention!'

Both Roger and Keith would have been horrified to learn that someone was watching the watchers. Shaun Bu'mole had been busy. Shaun had discovered a carton of several hundred tiny spy cameras in a unit on the little industrial estate. He'd had to rig a series of battery-operated relays around the town as he couldn't piggyback onto wi-fi now. To his great delight, all those hours on YouTube were paying dividends.
The integrated system he'd created now worked perfectly, and he had views of Sedgewood from virtually anywhere anybody went now, including Roger and Keith in the police station.

A few members of the congregation had attempted to leave town again. Those who had initially disappeared had begun to return. Everyone told the same story.
You could go anywhere, but when you needed supplies,

you could only go to places you'd already visited before the changes.

Jim and Doreen Tinker had made it all the way to their holiday cottage in Cornwall, but only by stopping at petrol stations and shops they'd used in the past. Driving had been simple, there wasn't anyone else on the roads. They'd been making good progress until they'd tried visiting the huge shopping complex just off the M5 at Bristol.
Neither Jim or Doreen had been inside before, and they thought this would be a fantastic opportunity to load the car with free bounty.
From the outside, the signs and carparks were just as they remembered them, inside however, was completely devoid of anything, including any internal walls. It was eerie, and the Tinkers had driven away again quickly, not stopping until they arrived at Bridgewater Services, their regular stop.
At Bridgewater, the filling station shop had been full of stock, just as they remembered it.
They continued south, past Taunton and then Exeter, too nervous now to deviate from the route they'd travelled before.
There were sheep in the fields and birds overhead, but there weren't any cars, and there wasn't a trace of another living person.
On arriving in Polperro, they were able to drive right down into the heart of the village.
Their beloved little cottage was exactly as they'd left it just a few months previously, but apart from the omnipresent gulls, it was silent.

They decided to have a quick look around the usually cheerful hub of the village.

The lights were on in the post office, and the bakery window displayed an array of pasties, loaves, and cakes. The shops were as they remembered them, there was plenty of stock on display and everything looked exactly as it had on their last visit.

When they'd tentatively peered in a few of the cottage windows on Quay Road, they'd been horrified to discover the same empty shells as elsewhere, devoid of all signs of life or people.

Jim had suggested they go to their favourite pub by the harbour. They'd been there many times before and had always enjoyed a warm welcome. It was their away-from-home-local.

Jim, before the changes, had been just a few years away from retirement, and once his services were no longer needed for pest control in Sedgewood, the Tinkers had planned to move properly. They loved Polperro, they'd had so many happy times there.

The door of the Blue Peter had swung open, they immediately noticed that the fire wasn't lit this time. The lights were on and the fridges hummed gently, but there was no familiar smiling face behind the welcoming bar waiting to greet them.

As they stepped inside, the bar echoed with only the sound of their footsteps, their breathing, and the soft breaking of waves in the quiet outer harbour.

Jim called out a hopeful 'Hello?' and had waited a few

moments before hesitantly stepping behind the bar and pouring himself a pint of the Blue's own ale. He rummaged around in a fridge and found a bottle of dry white wine to offer to Doreen.

'I'm going to need a glass love' Doreen said nervously 'although I'm not far off just swigging from the bottle.'

Jim returned with a brief flicker of a smile 'It wouldn't be the first time eh?' he attempted to wink, but the situation was just too surreal.

Sedgewood had been weird at first, but he'd quietly been happy that so many of the people he used to interact with had gone.

The reason most of them called Jim in with his specialist skills, was that he often used to deliberately introduce cockroaches and rats into those locations in the first place. He'd use live traps in one location, and then to guarantee the next customer, go and release his prizes near the home or office of whoever had ticked him off most recently.

In Sedgewood, Jim had felt constantly on edge. His rat phobia didn't help, and as a pest control specialist, he knew where they were, and approximately how many of them there were too. There were a lot more than most people realised. His incessant fear made him constantly irritable. Now though, in his beloved escape place, everything felt wrong.

As he stepped back out from behind the bar, even not paying felt wrong, but what else could he do?

They sat quietly at their usual table for a few minutes and then Doreen said in a nervous voice 'I don't expect they'd mind if we lit the fire do you?'

'Look!' Jim gasped and pointed at the chalkboard on the wall beside the fireplace.

'Live Music this Saturday March 20th with Dew Barf.'

It was almost December now. That was exactly what the board had said the last time they'd been there.

Jim had begun sobbing.

The couple had drunk themselves to staggering stage with barely a word spoken between them.

When they could drink no more, they stumbled back through the deserted village to their beloved refuge.

In the morning, they'd stocked up on free pasties from the bakery window, and driven back to Sedgewood, through mist and driving rain, as quickly as they could.

The first person they met on their return was Renfield. He listened intently to their story, and then asked if he could write a song about it.

Miranda and Elaine chatted casually as Miranda prepared her favourite blend of coffee beans. The kitchen slowly filled with their rich, velvety aroma.

Taking a seat next to her friend, Miranda pulled her notebook towards her and clicked the shortcut to Facebook. She clicked again on the friends request.

"Here he is, Andrew Morton" she began scrolling down through his posts. There wasn't much to see, vet jokes mostly.

"Well at least it looks as if he can laugh at himself" Elaine offered, "How about his photo's?"

Miranda scrolled back up and clicked on the section marked Andrews Photos.

They were surprised to learn that before he'd been a vet, Andrew had been a medicine sans frontiers doctor. "Oh look, he's worked all over the world by the looks of things." Miranda was clearly surprised. She'd already pigeon-holed Andrew Morton in the 'Berk' category, now she was going to have to review her opinion.

They carried on scrolling through his photo's. There was a series of Andrew with an older lady which when they clicked on them, turned out to be his mum. They were obviously close, and when she'd died, Andrew, from his posts, had been heartbroken. He'd been in the Middle East at the time, about five years ago, desperately trying to help the innocent civilian casualties of American and British bombing.

They carried on looking, going further back now. Andrew had been a secondary school boy who by the looks of things, had worked in animal shelters while putting himself through his doctors training.

"I'm really beginning to warm to him." Elaine had said after they'd been examining the profile for half an hour and following links and comments on the photos.

Miranda reluctantly had to agree. Perhaps Andrew Morton wasn't so bad after all. "But what about the incident on Council Tossing Day?" she asked her friend.

"I just don't know, perhaps he's just not good at holding his beer?" Elaine suggested.

"That's not an excuse is it? If alcohol makes people lechy, then perhaps they shouldn't drink at all." Miranda answered with a finality Elaine knew well.

"Well perhaps you should give him the benefit of the doubt? Why don't we have a look and see whether he posted anything about that weekend?"

Miranda clicked on the newsfeed and began scrolling back through Andrews posts to June.

They both gasped when the long post about the weekend came up. There was no photo, just this.

Andrew Morton. June 22nd.

'I'm absolutely mortified by the events of the weekend and I wish to apologise whole heartedly to absolutely anyone and everyone I might have seen on Sunday.'

Miranda and Elaine looked at one another, 'Oh my....'

The post went on

'My behaviour was probably outrageous, inappropriate, and quite frankly, unacceptable. I know now from the results of the blood test I had on Sunday evening that I had unknowingly ingested a large quantity of a type of poisonous, hallucinogenic mushroom, as had at least three other customers in the pub we'd visited.

This I have been told, was probably dropped into my glass in powdered form. The police are investigating.

I truly don't know what I did, but apparently all of us who were affected were awful.

I don't know who punched me, but from the sound of the description of the way I was out of control, I must have deserved it.

I'd like to thank whoever it was and buy him a pint, because I passed out immediately afterwards, which led to me getting the treatment I so urgently needed.

I truly pray that this doesn't completely sour the milk for me in this beautiful little town now.

Mortified!

There were three sad face emojis at the end of the post.

"He doesn't use emojis on any of the other posts." Miranda remarked.

Let's have a look at the comments? Elaine responded.

There were almost a hundred of them.

Lots of Andrews friends had expressed their shock and then their condolences. Down past the midway point, the comments extended across several days rather than hours. One from Andrew said "Just had the CCTV report from the pub and police. Think they caught the little git who doped us."

There were many calls of 'I hope they bung him in prison.' A little further down the page there was another cause to gasp.

'Oh my word, I've seen the CCTV myself now. I saw what

I did. I was hit by a woman; it was completely justified. The local coppers say she wasn't anyone they recognised. Whoever she is, I'm so ashamed, it wasn't her fault.'

"Oh my god Miranda" Elaine took her friends hand in her own.

"Yes I know. Just give me a minute, I need to process that."

"The local coppers say she wasn't anyone they recognised?" Elaine repeated. "Really?" she laughed, Miranda, you're probably the most recognisable woman in the whole town."

"I bet that was Dan, bless him, he never said anything. Oh god, I didn't know there was CCTV"

Elaine laugh-snorted "HA! Hahahaha, anyone else might have said Oh god I'm so sorry I whacked him?"

"Oh hell no" Miranda answered just as firmly as always. Just because he'd been spiked doesn't make it okay, he bloody deserved it and that's a fact!"

"Hmm, so what are you going to do about his friend request? It's a small town and you're bound to bump into him. You'll definitely see him when you have to go to the vets."

Miranda thought about it.

"You're right of course, as usual" she added smiling at her friend.

"I need a few days to mull it over. I was going to just ignore him."

"Ignore? That's new, I thought you generally blocked people?"

For an instant in her mind's eye, Miranda saw the big BLOCKED button, but of course Elaine only meant the conventional way…didn't she?

Mercifully, the spell was broken by a familiar knock on the door as Dan arrived to collect Nigel.

A week had passed. Andrew Morton was just about to clamber into the shower in his little rented cottage, when his phone beeped with the instantly recognisable tone he'd programmed in.

Veterinary Emergency!

Another one? It felt as though Andrew hadn't stopped for days, and indeed he hadn't.

When he'd taken on the role of senior practitioner in Sedgewood, he'd also volunteered to be on call for emergencies for the PDSA and for the local badger, fox, and hedgehog rescue group.

Andrews experiences overseas with Medicine sans frontiers had left him traumatised. Consequently, after twelve years, he'd retrained. He was still driven by compassion, but he needed a completely different set of patients and circumstances. He had never imagined that so many animals would need his help.

In the last seventy-two hours, Andrew had spent less than eight hours either asleep or at home. The beeper just kept going.

He grabbed the phone and looked at the message. Another young fox had been clipped by a car. This was the time of year when the young foxes, no longer cubs, had to set off into the world to find their own place in it. It was a brutal time for all sorts of animals. Some of the lucky ones had found their way to Andrews surgical table where his brilliant skill set had performed miracles.

The young fox would have to be sedated. One of the staff at the practice was already taking the necessary steps. He showered as quickly as he could, and then still only half dressed, rushed out to his little mini. The exhaust had started to come apart but he just hadn't had time to fix it. It was going to make a terrible noise, but that couldn't be helped.

He was fatigued already, but as always, he knew that adrenaline and caffeine would get him through. He knew he was driving a little faster than he usually would at just over twenty-two miles an hour, but a life was at stake.

As he approached the main road through the town, he realised that the schools were just finishing for the day. The fastest way to the practice at this time of the afternoon was down by the Forty and then along Cedar Avenue. Seeing the road ahead was clear, he pushed the mini up another notch.

When he trundled passed Miranda, Andrew was travelling at twenty-six miles an hour.

The exhaust made a noise like a world war two Hurricane. To Miranda, it was is if he were flying along.

Andrew didn't see her, but Miranda, who was on her way to meet Sam at the marketplace, had heard the approaching roar from the buckled exhaust long before the little car appeared.

'Another idiot.' She mumbled to herself, and then to her surprise, recognised the face of the driver from the Facebook profile she'd continued to study on and off for the last week. She'd never have imagined him driving such a modest little car.

Oblivious to the reason for his haste, Miranda continued

muttering to herself.

"Well now, if that's how you drive mister Morton, perhaps Sedgewood can manage without you."

She took out her phone and looked at the Sedgewood veterinary practice website. There were four vets in all, Miranda already knew three of them.

Yes, she decided, Sedgewood could probably manage without Andrew Morton.

Unseen by anyone, Freya smiled and nodded to herself approvingly. 'I think she's really getting the hang of this now.'

If tonight was the night Andrew Morton was going, then she needed to have a quick chat with Bee.

She made a quick call on the ether-net. "Bee? Bee? Are you receiving me?"

At Doggyopolis, Bee was enjoying watching Kevin and Nigel romping around the Chase-me rabbit track.

Bee was pondering the fact that as the Blocked World Sedgewood reflected the original little town in every way except the human inhabitants, over in New Sedgewood, identical dogs were running happily around Doggyopolis. The law of superposition meant that at this very moment, Kevin, and Nigel , were enjoying tearing around the track after the stuffed toy with equal joy and enthusiasm in both worlds.

Of course in the source world, Dan Rapier would take the boys home at the end of the day. In New Sedgewood, Kevin and Nigel would just go home of their own accord. The nature of quantum entanglement meant that what

Kevin and Nigel experienced in the source world, also flowed through to them here in New Sedgewood. Their food dishes were filled at the same times, the doors were opened to let them gallop around the gardens, and although their humans weren't physically present in Blocked World, both dogs could feel their people and feel their love and affection.

For the New Sedgewood expressions of Kevin and Nigel, everything was the same, almost.
The one exception the guides had allowed was that over where all the blocked people had appeared, Nigel was allowed to chase Roger Parkinson. Nigel had enjoyed that. Bee laughed to herself. If Nigel ever had caught Roger, he wouldn't have known what to do next anyway. Dear Nigel didn't have an iota of malice in him, he just enjoyed the chase.
The guides had all agreed that watching Rogers desperate attempts to flee on the half dozen occasions they'd met so far, had been hilarious. Nobody liked Roger.

She was brought out of her reverie when Freya's thoughtform came to her in shouty.
"Bee?......Bee?....Bee? Oh-forfucksake….. BOUDICA! CAN YOU FRIGGIN HEAR ME?"
The former warrior queen of the Iceni snapped abruptly back on duty and bilocated to Freyas side.
"I'm really sorry love, I was getting completely immersed. Those two boys are so beautiful."
Freya looked at her fellow Spirit guide and said
"It's going to be the Morton incident tonight, so we're bot

on tomorrow."

Bee seemed to momentarily lose a little of her poise.

"Oh god" she groaned "I can't tell you how much I've been dreading this."

Freya reached out a kind hand to comfort Bee.

"You know it's all going to work out though, yeah?"

"I know, but I'd rather do anything other than do it this way. Couldn't we have sacrificed Roger Parkinson or something instead?"

"I asked the boss that in our session last week. He said…" Boudica finished the sentence for her in a slightly whiney tone "He said everything's unfolding exactly as it ought to." And then, "You know, he might be the boss, but he really pisses me off sometimes."

A gentle voice whispered in Bee's ear. "I heard that" and then audible to both of them. "What must be, must be"

As if by magic, Norman appeared. "Oh Hi Miss Boudica, hi Miss Freya." Norman tipped his hat to the ladies and then looked up and said, "I'm really sorry your almightyworshipfullsupremenesess sir, but I've been trying to get through to you?"

The voice of the boss came through to all three of them. "Very well Norman, come with me and we'll go through the brief just one more time."

And then Norman and the boss were gone.

"Poor Norman, he is struggling a bit" offered Bee sympathetically.

"I know, but would you want Roger Parkinson as your first job, slimy little toad he is. If he'd been my charge, I'd have let him climb into that hippopotamus enclosure when he went to the zoo that time"

Bee laughed and agreed. "Yes I read his life plan too. I think I'd have probably left plenty of knitting needles lying around for him to stuff into electricity sockets when he was toddling." She gave one of her dazzling smiles and said "Freya, do you think you could help me with something? It's to do with, you know, what's coming?"

Freya had already picked up telepathically what was coming. "Oo, I think that's a really great idea. I can see why you wited until the boss was distracted. Good old Norman."

They linked arms to shift dimensions to New Sedgewood. As they were about to go, Freya looked at her friend and winked and said "You know actually Bee, between you and me, I think Norman is really handsome. Do you think it would be a possibility? You know, a man like Norman and a girl like me?"

Andrew Morton changed into a fresh set of scrubs. This was at almost five o'clock. The arrivals hadn't stopped. He'd saved the young fox and repaired the broken pelvis, making sure the young fellow was properly immobilised until the bones had fused again.

Next had been a pigmy goat which had almost asphyxiated on a lump of still wrapped brie it had swallowed whole, after learning how to jump onto his human friends kitchen worktop.

By the time that was done, it was time for the usual evening surgery. Andrew had examined and treated a steady flow of cats, dogs, birds reptiles and rodents. Nothing from the usual repertoire was absent.

After the last patient had left, the phone had immediately begun beeping again. It was yet another diverted call from the emergency number. It was a little before 9pm now. Two of his colleagues were already out on farms dealing with separate incidents involving a pig and a wallaby.

This time when Andrew answered, the emergency, thankfully, was a spoof call. Andrew could tell it was a group of sniggering lads, probably in a pub somewhere. He played along anyway. "Okay, yes, a Giraffe, appears to have a sore throat. Sedgewood animal land. Yes okay, goodnight lads."

He put the phone by the sink in the little washroom next to the theatre and began one last scrub. Hopefully, he could go home now.

He gathered up his jacket and freshly sterilised phone, and having locked the main surgery doors, decided he'd stop off at Joy's shop on his way home for a bottle of wine. Usually in these circumstances, he'd get the cork out, pour a glass, sit down in his favourite armchair to drink it, and immediately become unconscious. He forced himself to alertness and slowly drove the short distance to the little general store. He was too late. Just as he was about to clamber out of the mini, the shop lights went off. He slumped back heavily in the driver's seat, let out a loud frustrated sigh and fell promptly asleep.

He was still asleep when Miranda Boycott imagined the big red button again. Miranda had spent the evening questioning whether a dose of mushrooms would really make someone behave that way. She knew her dislike of the man was irrational, especially having studied his profile in detail now.

Andrew Morton was apparently, quite a decent chap. He did worthwhile work, he was well liked by his friends, he underplayed his achievements and it turned out he was an enthusiastic gardener. He and Sam would have probably made easy friends.

The Trouble was, with Miranda, first impressions stuck, and Miranda had never been especially forgiving. Besides, she told herself, if he drove like a lunatic the way he had done this afternoon, it was only a matter of time until harm came as a result of it.

"Yes Mr Morton, you can go" she whispered to herself in the dark, and he did.

The first two people to become aware of Andrews arrival, were Roger Parkinson and Taxi Keith. They'd both witnessed the little mini materialise on the screens in the police station as they'd been watching a few nocturnal residents creeping around the town. Old habits were definitely hard to break they'd agreed, watching some of the peculiar pastimes of their fellows.

The arrival of the mini had caused great excitement for Roger and Keith. They had looked at one another in astonishment, and then Keith had suggested "I think I know what it is now, it's a portal!"
"I think our troubadour might have been on to something."
They'd rushed outside to where Keiths Blocked World version of his taxi was parked, and wasted no time in making their way to where the little mini had appeared.

The troubadour, as Renfield had been nicknamed, had written a song about worlds besides worlds and wishing he could step through a mirror to get home.
Kristen had ordered him to leave her flat now that he'd outlived his usefulness and everything was free anyway. The last thing she wanted to listen to, was the incessant plucking as he worked on his latest creation. It had been completely different when they'd first met and she'd harboured the delusion that she was going to become a pop star.

Renfield the troubadour had taken to playing in the heart of New Sedgewood whenever the weather was clement.

Some of the bored residents would come and listen to his latest offerings. He was actually quite good when he was on his own. When Kristen had first met him, they'd performed a few duets which would have appalled the most dedicated of caterwaulers. After several weeks in this strange new version of Sedgewood, Renfield's songs had suggested a number of theories about why the changes had occurred, a great many of them based on Star Trek storylines.

Keith and Roger had been among the listeners, and like everyone else, wanted to know exactly what was going on. Right now, they had an advantage. They could probably get to the new arrival before anyone else did, and before Renfield wrote another song.

Andrew was rudely awoken by an incessant tapping on the window. A voice said "Hey" Mate! Have you just arrived?" A second voice joined the first. "Can you tell us where you were just now?"

A befuddled Andrew opened the door and climbed out onto the roadside to greet the faces of the two men who were making the enquiries.

He recognised them immediately. He'd seen them in dozens of newspapers and on the news.

"You're Roger aren't you? And you're Kieth."

"Erm, yes mate, do we know each other? Have you just arrived?"

Andrew was exhausted and confused.

"Look, sorry chaps, but I just need to go home." Against their almost hysterical appeals, he clambered back into the mini and drove off. Roger and Keith decided to follow. "I' keep the lights off" Keith said, "I don't want to spook him."

Andrew didn't notice anything at all strange on the way home, and mercifully, he didn't encounter anyone else. Where on earth had those two appeared from? Andrew was too tired to think. He stumbled in through his front door, kicking off his shoes as he went, and went straight upstairs to bed.

As Andrew began snoring deeply, Roger and Kieth looked at the outside of his house from the taxi.
"Perhaps he'll be ready to talk in the morning?" Keith suggested.
"Aye, I reckon. I remember when the changes first happened to me, I slept solid for about six hours, even though it was night-time." Roger replied and then added "You go on back if you like mate, I think I might have a little look around just until he wakes up." Old habits did indeed die hard.

A week had passed. In Sedgewood, the police had yet another mystery on their hands. One of the vets had vanished, the new one who everybody seemed to like.

Miranda had been careful to avoid Dan Rapier, and she was beginning to feel sharp twinges of guilt as she watched the television news and listened to the reports on the radio. More of Andrews past had come to light, and it painted a picture of a kind, caring, compassionate man who had spent his life putting the needs of others before his own.

By Friday, Miranda was wrestling with her own conscience so much, that she could barely concentrate on the article she was writing. She went back to the beginning to start again. 'Should you put up with manipulative behaviour by family members?'
was the title. Right now, Miranda was thinking about her own actions. Just how manipulative had it been to make all those people vanish? Then again she thought, until the case of Andrew Morton, there wasn't one individual she'd sent to…wherever, who she ever wanted to see again anyway. She put her head in her hands. "Oh god. What have I done? And where the hell do they go anyway?"
This was the first time Miranda had genuinely begun thinking about where the people she'd blocked might have ended up. "Oh my god" she kept mumbling to herself, having visions of people vaporising before her eyes. If they went to Hell, she rationalised, then that was surely their own fault, if there even was such a place? Perhaps she'd just sped up the process a little?

There was a familiar knock at the door. Nigel jumped up to do his duty and go and welcome the visitor. Mirandas heart lept into her mouth.

Dan.

Oh damn! She'd been so caught up in her conflicted feelings, she'd completely forgotten that today was the boys now regular trip to Doggyopolis.

She did her best to compose herself as she went to answer. "Hi Dan" she leaned forward to give him their customary hug. "I'm so sorry, I was miles away" She answered truthfully "I'd completely forgotten, and I'm not getting on very well with the article I'm supposed to be working on." Stick to the facts and avoid anything to do with the vet her internal monologue whispered.

And then before she could stop herself "Anyway, how are you?" Miranda instantly wished she could just vanish into the carpet. 'Just like all those people seemed to have done…' the little voice whispered again. She could feel herself flushing, she rapidly bent down on the pretence of making a fuss of Kevin as the two brothers exchanged excited doggy greetings and took turns to sniff each other's bums.

Thankfully, Dan was paying more attention to the two spaniels than he was to Miranda.

"Oh we're okay thanks" Dan always included Kevin. "Bit of a strange one at work again though. I expect you've heard what's happened?"

Miranda stood up again and did her best to look innocent. "Oh yes, terrible isn't it? What do you think happened to him? I'll just grab Nigel's lead."

She began fumbling among the coat hooks.

"So far, we don't know any more about this one than we do about any of the others." He took the lead as she turned back to face him.

"Miranda, I hadn't said anything before, but you know you'd met him don't you?"

Miranda could feel her blood pressure rise a few more bars. Before she could say anything Dan continued, "Although you wouldn't have known it was him, he was dressed as Trevor Cooper on Council tossing day" Dan gave her the broadest of grins and said "Can't tell you how many times we watched the replay down at the station. You really caught him a beauty"

Miranda knew there was no point in denying anything. Anyway, her public interactions had been a hundred percent innocent, apart from the fact that she'd felled Andrew with a move Bruce Lee would have been proud of. She decided to be open before any questions came her way.

"Yes we met a few weeks ago actually, although to be completely truthful, I had no idea he was the Trevor.

"I'd better get going." Dan indicated the spaniels who were obviously eager to go for their adventure.

"Perhaps we could have a chat later when I bring Nigel back? It's ages since I caught up with Sam."

"Yes, certainly. I'd love that, and so would Sam. He ought to be back by four-ish. What time do you think you'll be back Dan?"

"Oh, you know the boys" he smiled again "As long as it takes to wear them out"

"That could be a while then." Miranda leaned forward and gave him a peck on the cheek. "Thanks Dan, Nigel loves his trips out with you. See you later."

Miranda had watched Dan close the gate and had gone back to her writing desk.

She really needed to talk to someone, who could she tell?

In one of those moments the Spirit guides were in charge of, the phone rang. It was Elaine. "Hi Miranda, are you busy?"

"A bit, but I've hit a bit of a wall and I'm a bit distracted to be honest."

"I'm a bit stuck myself, and I keep thinking about that poor man."

Miranda felt as though the top of her head was about to pop off. "You mean Andrew Morton? Yes I know. I've been thinking a lot about that here too."

Miranda glanced at the clock. She had just over three hours until Sam was due back.

Dan, if he kept to the previous routines, would be about an hour later. Perhaps she could cram it all in?

"Elaine, I could really use a chat, can I come round?"

"Ah, bit of a problem, we're having those new carpets fitted today, Tom's here and three carpet fitters. Why it takes three is beyond me. I could come to you though."

Oh god. Bless you Elaine. Can you ask Tom to pick you up later? This is going to need a glass or two."

"Oh Miranda, my poor love, what's wrong? I'll be there in fifteen minutes."

Andrew Morton had been in New Sedgewood for a week. On his first day, he'd awoken to discover Roger Parkinson and Taxi Keith asleep in a taxi parked immediately outside his house.

Unusually, his phone hadn't beeped yet this morning. There was usually something urgent he'd have to go in ear for. Last Saturday, he'd had to rush in to rehydrate a little Magellan penguin which according to the family who had brought the poor little thing to the surgery, 'Must have climbed into the camper when we were at the safari park.' He checked for messages. There was no service.

He was scheduled for the Saturday morning surgery in just over an hour. He showered and then to his considerable relief, dressed in fresh clothing for the first time in four days. Andrew was no stranger to this kind of austerity. Of course, In a clinical environment, he had full scrubs and protective clothing anyway. With a steady procession of emergencies though, the needs of the patients had always overridden the need for a fresh pair of socks.

Breakfast consisted of a full pack of crumpets, liberally drowned in butter, and three large mugs of coffee.

When he turned to lock his front door, the taxi was still there, along with the obviously sleeping figures of Roger and Keith.

It was a beautiful late autumn morning. He wasn't on call until Tuesday now so he wouldn't need the car. Andrew decided to walk.

He'd gone less than a hundred paces before he began to notice something was very odd. Andrew had worked in war zones and he recognised the silence. Where was everyone?

He strained to listen. Where were the cars and the buses? Why weren't there any people on the streets. As he approached the turning where Joys little shop was, he was relieved to see that the lights were on. When he stepped inside, he soon discovered that no one was home. Other Sedgewood residents had said this of Joy on several occasions.

Andrew was deeply unsettled, but he pressed onto the surgery anyway. He had a job to do, and people, and more importantly their pets, needed him.
When he arrived at the surgery, again, the lights were on, but there wasn't anybody there.
He walked around the building three times, shouting now to see whether anyone would answer his calls.
The surgery's computers were all turned on, but there was clearly no internet service.
Bewildered, he plonked himself in a chair at the reception desk and picked up the phone. Something was obviously very badly wrong. It was time to call the police.
He might as well have tried to lasso a cloud.

At nine O'clock, when the waiting room was usually full of anxious owners and an assortment of fur and feathers, not one person had appeared. Andrew had waited, feeling a growing sense of impending doom.
Half past nine took an age to arrive. Ten O'clock took even longer.
At last, he could stand it no more, and decided to walk the short distance across the recreation ground and go directly to the police station.

There were no cars, and at first Andrew had thought there were no people either. It was like being in the opening scene of some terrible dystopian film where he was the only person left on the planet.

Then he heard the yelling. Running at full pelt, as if his life depended on it, was a camouflaged man. Just a few paces behind him was a beautiful springer spaniel. Andrew thought he recognised the man from the taxi from the night before. He again recalled all the television and newspaper coverage. Yes, he was pretty certain that he was looking at Roger Parkinson. This had to be worth a photograph. He delved into his pocket and manged to capture a short sequence as Roger and the spaniel carried on tearing down the street.

"Why can't you just leave me alone" he heard Roger wail in the distance.

For the next few minutes as he walked down Honey Lane, there were no sounds other than the birds and the crunching of fallen leaves from underfoot.

One of Sedgewood's most beautiful surviving medieval buildings stood at the end. Once it had been a pub, today, only the name remained. The Old Beehive Inn.

Coming from the open windows of a huge conservatory which had been tastefully added to the end of the building, came the strumming of a guitar, and a few experimental lyrics.

"Can't get back, I feel so bad
Can't get back, I feel so lost
I should be happy where I'm at

But I don't think,
… mumble, mumble…bear the cost….mmm,
whoo, Whoo, ooooo.

Andrew stopped at the gate to gaze in. The songwriter was obviously engrossed and it took Andrew a few attempts to get his attention. At first he'd waved from the gate. Next he'd tried calling, but not loudly, not wanting to disturb anyone who might be asleep. Andrew worked that way. Anyone else would have just gone in or started shouting straight away.

Eventually, as the whoo-ooing, mumble mumble whoo-ooooo had continued, Andrew opened the gate and went right up to the conservatory window. The scrunching of the gravel finally got the troubadour's attention.

"Hi, I'm sorry to disturb you" Andrew began.

The troubadour wasted no time at all.

"Oh crickey fella, have you just arrived?" he quickly put the guitar back on a stand and hurried over to the glass door to beckon Andrew in.

"When did you get here mate?"

Andrew looked puzzled.

"What do you mean? I've been here for months. I'm the new vet up at the surgery?"

"Oh not there mate. I mean when did you get here?"

The troubadour pointed at the floor. He could see Andrew didn't understand.

"You'd better sit-down fella. Would you like a brew?" he pointed at a mug on the glass topped table.

Everything looked clean enough, and anyway, where Andrew had been in his life, he was probably immune to virtually every kind of bacteria on the planet. He nodded and said "Erm, yes, okay, thanks." Then he added "I'm pretty certain I've just seen Roger Parkinson being chased by a dog."

"Oh yeah? Probably. Roger's been here longer than any of us. I don't think that springer likes him. He said at one of the meetings that it's the Boycotts dog, but they're not here" the troubadour paused briefly and stared out of the window while he thought about things.

Eventually he said. "I'm not surprised the dog chases him, he's a right Billy no mates that one.

The irony was completely lost on the would-be singer songwriter. Before Andrew could comment he added, "It's really weird you know. Everyone's cats and dogs are here, but not the people. I've got no idea how it works, but they just seem to look after themselves."

Andrew was even more confused now. What the hell was going on?

"I'll pop the kettle on, have a seat mate." The troubadour amiably indicated an armchair.

The tea was remarkably good. Andrew sat facing the troubadour now and felt it was time for a formal introduction. He extended his hand saying, "I'm Andrew, Andrew Morton." With a smile, the troubadour offered his hand in return, hardly anybody ever asked his name. "I'm Martin." and then "I'm guessing you've just arrived. I'd better explain a bit."

Andrew involuntarily wiped his hand on his trousers. The setting was clean, but it didn't look as if personal hygiene was very high on Martins list of priorities.

Over the next hour, Martin the troubadour explained, based on the stories he'd gathered, that in the beginning, it had just been Roger and Keith. Then it was the congregation, and then he had arrived along with Kristen and Toya.

"I've seen all of you in the papers" Andrew had explained in return.

Martin went on to describe the way the shops replenished themselves and that apart from the landscape, only things someone in the group of misfits had experienced previously, existed here.

Things had become increasingly factionalised, but Martin had also explained why nobody wanted to leave.

"There's a kind of uneasy peace hanging over the town" he explained.

Andrew's usual metal fortitude was being tested to the limits. "Is it safe to go out and walk around?" he'd asked.

"Oh yeah, you can drive too. The petrol in Gary's Garage never runs out. For some reason though, most of the locals seem to go around on bicycles now. I think it's because they're quieter. Nobody makes a lot of noise here now. I'm getting to quite like it really."

"Oh, was it a problem then?" Andrew was keen to learn as much as he possibly could.

"Well, when we got here, apparently most of it had begun to settle down. There was quite a lot of vandalism at first. But seeing as everything just kept repairing itself overnight, there's no point. It's like there's some sort of automatic reset. The seasons change, but the day-to-day things stay the same.

Andrew needed to see for himself and said so.

"Well, you'll be okay, but don't be surprised when they all jump on you and start asking a million questions. They're all desperate to know what's happening back at…" Martin paused for a few moments before saying sadly, "…home."

By the time Andrew emerged from the Old Beehive Inn, Taxi Keith had already spread word of the new arrival. Roger had gone back to his lair back at the telephone exchange. He would have made an ideal partner for Nosferatu-Kristen. Neither of them liked being out in daylight, and both of them were equally loathed by the remaining population of New Sedgewood. Even Toya had finally worked out just how much Kristen would try to manipulate people, and she was beginning to suspect that Kristen was the main reason they found themselves here now.

In the absence of phones, the residents had discovered that baby monitors could be used for communication. The little industrial unit where Shaun Bu'mole had found his little cameras, had been thoroughly ransacked.

Messages flew across the little town and Andrew, despite his best attempts to evade being seen, was witnessed returning to his own house. A crowd gathered outside.

Malcolm Turner, former keyholder for The Church of the Eternally Confused, was no more popular than any of the other residents, but he was also, by a margin, probably less disliked.

Malcolm was a computer software engineer. Malcolms littl

quirk had been to repair peoples PC's at their homes, and secretly upload a virus which would keep him coming back for months afterwards.

Malcolm had been caught and had been called to account for his actions in court. He'd pleaded temporary insanity and claimed that he was seeking salvation at the Church of the Eternally Confused.

Most of the congregation already knew that Malcolm and his wife Cathy, had mostly joined the church so that Malcolm could expand his other little business, the one where he imported a certain range of 'intimate, personal items.'

Noone had ever been able to find out exactly what those had been, although to the congregation, it had all sounded rather exciting.

Malcolm had been elected as spokesman, and so he strode up to the door and knocked loudly. Andrew had ignored it at first, but soon realised he wouldn't get any peace until he'd responded.

"We'd just like to ask a few questions." Malcolm had told him.

Andrew had reluctantly agreed and then said "I really need a beer. Look, there's a big room at the back of the Wizards, shall we all go up there?"

It was agreed. For Andrew, it was going to be another incredibly long and sleepless night.

Over several hours and numerous pints of Ale, Andrew had answered a barrage of questions.

As he'd been in Sedgewood since just before Council

Tossing weekend, Andrew had been privy to an extensive body of media coverage. From his version of Sedgewood, he knew most of the faces, and a good number of the names. He also knew some of the less glamorous stories of the people he was currently sharing the Wizards Staff function room with. He did his best to remain diplomatic and gentile. Thank god for his training in bedside manner. By the time people began leaving in the small, dark hours of the morning, Andrew was once again exhausted, and still nobody had any real answers about how they'd arrived here.

Andrew went back to his own home where he spent an unrestful night dreaming about mirrors and trying to pass himself through them.

Elaine true to her word, had arrived quarter of an hour after Miranda had put the phone down. She was clutching a clanking carrier bag. "Stopped in at Joys" she explained as she took her coat off. "Where are we then?" She could see how pale and worried Miranda looked.

Miranda indicated the lounge where she'd just lit the wood burner. "I think it's probably best if we go in here. You're going to need to be comfortable for this."

Elaine wanted to express her concern but she knew she just needed to sit back and listen for a while.

Miranda disappeared into the kitchen.

"No Nigel?" Elaine asked, and then immediately wished she hadn't in case something bad had happened.

"Not today" came the reply "He's out with 'Quick-as -you-like, they've all gone to Doggyopolis"

Elaine breathed a sigh of relief.

Miranda came back with her two biggest wine glasses.

"Oh dear, that serious?"

"To be honest Elaine, I think you'll think I'm a bit made. I'm sure there has to be a rational explanation, but it goes like this."

Miranda filled the glasses and looked at her friend earnestly and began.

"You know when you block someone on social media……"

For the next hour, Elaine barely said a word.

Thank goodness is was only this. If Miranda really had done these things, Elaine couldn't see any problem with them at all so far. Especially now that so many of the unsavoury aspects of these peoples characters had come to light in the media.

When Miranda got to the part where she'd Blocked Kristen, Toya and Renfield, Elaine finally ventured an opinion.

"Oh good. I've hated that smarmy little blond bitch ever since she first arrived here. That Toya is a waste of space too. All tit's, cockney accent, and big car. What does she need a tank like that for anyway?

I tried talking to her once, she thinks she's really bright." Elaine laughed "I've seen turds which are brighter than she is." Miranda nodded, Elaine continued

"That was evil what they did to that beautiful laburnum, and unforgivable. I loved seeing that tree every spring. Really spiteful! Nasty little cows." She took a gulp of her wine and said, "Go on?"

Miranda took another mouthful from her glass and said, "I blocked Andrew Morton."

"Oh? When?

Oh god Elaine, haven't you seen the news? It's everywhere, and social media, surely you must have seen he's gone? You said so on the phone?"

Elaine shook her head. "Haven't seen any internet at all since last Saturday. Our hub overheated and died.

We decided to make the most of it and while I've been working on my book, Toms been busy decorating.

It's been lovely actually. We've really reconnected this week me and Tom. We've had the wood burner lit every night, we've taken it in turns to cook, and we've either sat and read, or we've talked, actually talked, just like we used to."

"But you must have heard a radio or something?"

"Yes, only just though, you see neither of us has left the house in a week. Tom messaged the hub people on his phone, and apart from that, it's been like the Eighties in our house. That's why I rang, we just got all our connections back, and oh, yes, we'd only just heard"
"Miranda, don't hate me for asking this, but do you really think you can make people vanish? I mean, where do they go?"
Miranda exhaled deeply again and said ,"Well that's the question isn't it, where *do* they go?"
"Oh come on, even in your wildest imagination, you can't honestly believe you can make that happen? It's coincidence, pure coincidence" and then a little uncertainly "It has to be."

Miranda sat back in her chair and after a long pause said simply "Maybe"
They sat in silence for a while until Elaine sat up sharply. "I know, why don't we think of someone we both don't like, and you see whether you can block them?"
Miranda thought about it for a second and then said, "To be honest Elaine, I can think of quite a lot of people I'd like to send away, but what if it's someone decent? Someone like Andrew? I never meant to hurt anyone, I just wanted there to be a few less wankers in the world. I feel so bad about Andrew."

There was silence for another, long five minutes which Elaine finally broke again. " Have you tried to bring anyone back? You know, by unblocking them?"
Miranda didn't have time to answer, Elaine was visibly

excited now.

"What if it was somebody really horrible?"

"Like whom?" Miranda asked back.

"Oh I don't know. Oh, hang on, what about that politician, that wet fart that tried to do that celebrity thing?"

Miranda knew exactly who Elaine meant.

"Oh you mean Max Bancroft. Oh boy yes, he's a piece of work. I had to interview him once. He tried groping me."

"Right then, block him then. If it really is you, it'll soon be on the telly."

"How long have we got until Sam comes home?"

It was a little after two thirty. Plenty of time.

Miranda picked up the tv remote control saying "Righto, let's find the livestream from the House of Commons."

The television came to life and Mirada began flicking through channels until she found what she was looking for. It was a busy day in the House. Prime ministers question time was about to begin.

"There he is the odious little shit!" Elaine pointed excitedly at the screen and then looked at her friend. "Come on then witchy poo, do your stuff then."

Miranda looked uncertain.

Elaine encouraged her. "Look Miranda, what better way to show that it's just coincidence?"

Miranda acquiesced and sat back in her chair.

She closed her eyes and pictured Max Bancroft's piggy little face. She took a deep breath and visualised the big red button.

There was a barely audible sucking noise. Almost at once both Elaine shrieked and the noise from the screen burst out into pandemonium.

Elaine lapsed into silence for a few seconds and then turned to Miranda whose eyes were now fixed firmly on the chaos unfolding in Westminster.

"Oh my god Miranda, he vanished. It really is you."

Miranda looked at her friend again and said "Yeah, I know. Told you."

In a Blocked World version of the Palace of Westminster, a very confused, sleazy politician found himself suddenly all alone.

"That was amazing. Can you do it again? How about both party leaders this time?" Elaine could see a world of possibilities unfolding. She was excited.

Miranda was about to answer when there was a knock at the door.

"She rose to open it and said, "Whoever it is, I'll get rid of them quickly."

It was Dan Rapier. Miranda was shocked. In all the years they'd known one another, she had never seen him like this. He was ashen and his eyes were almost blood red. There was no doubt at all he'd been crying. Miranda was momentarily too stunned to speak.

"Miranda, oh my god I don't know how to say this. Something terrible has happened." Dan could barely speak. Miranda's first thought flew to Sam, and then she realised that Dan was alone. Neither of the spaniels was anywhere in sight.

Before she could ask anything Dan managed to say a few words between sobs. "You have to come with me now,

Nigel's badly hurt but there's a chance he'll be okay."
Dan indicated a taxi which was waiting on the kerbside.
Miranda wasted no time and reached up to grab her coat
while calling through to Elaine "I have to go. It's serious!"
She knew that Elaine would let herself out.

They hurried to the taxi and once the doors were closed
Miranda was finally able to ask in a rush "Oh god Dan,
what happened? You said Nigel's hurt? What about Kevin?
Is he okay?"

Dan looked utterly distraught; his face crumpled as he
barely managed to tell her in a low trembling voice
"Kevin's gone."

At the veterinary surgery, one of the kind nurses allowed Miranda to enter the room where Nigel, dear, sweet, beautiful Nigel, lay on a table covered with surgical sheets. He had two tubes of fluid running into his forelegs. Unseen beneath the lightweight sheets, another tube carrying donated dog blood was connected somehow.

The sight was shocking to Miranda. Mercifully, there was no visible sign of injury, although clearly something devastating had happened. Nigel's eyelids fluttered under the anaesthetic.

Dan Rapier had been too distressed to tell Miranda what had happened. Fortunately, the taxi driver who had witnessed the accident had been able to tell the medical staff what he'd witnessed.

The same kind taxi driver had gently picked up Kevin and put a blanket over him in the boot of his car. He'd driven carefully but as quickly as he could to deliver Dan and Nigel to the surgery and had then immediately offered to collect Miranda.

The veterinary nurse did her best to explain to Miranda. She already knew the two brother spaniels. "Apparently the boys were playing on the water slide when one of them, Kevin I think" she said sadly "spotted a fox crossing the road by the common. They just took off. There was nothing anyone could have done about it."

Miranda was sobbing herself now. She could guess what had happened.

Even though the mini-bus driver had slammed on his brakes, poor Kevin had taken the full force of the blow. "It was instant" the young woman explained compassionately.

"As for poor old Nigel there" she gestured the barely breathing spaniel "He rushed to his brothers side and was clipped by a car coming from the other direction." Then she added with obvious anger "Barry the taxi said the other driver just carried on, but he did get his number."

Miranda felt sick. Her poor beloved Nigel. And poor, heartbroken Dan. She couldn't bring herself to think of Kevin. And what would Sam do if Nigel didn't…Miranda crushed that thought immediately. The idea of losing Nigel was just too terrible.

"What's going to happen now?" she asked in an uncharacteristically small voice.

"We're waiting for Doctor Bennet to come over from Bumford. He's filling in for Mister Morton. I'm guessing you heard?"

"Mmm, yes" Miranda managed, and then asked "How is he? Is he going to be okay?"

The kind young nurse indicated a pair of chairs by the window. Miranda sat down heavily. The full enormity of blocking the person she most desperately needed in this moment, left her bereft with guilt and grief.

"Nigel took a very hard knock." The kind young woman decided to omit the fact that Nigel had been thrown over sixty feet through the air, before landing in the long roadside grass. She carried on. "We think he has some internal injuries and were just about to x-ray him. We knew you'd want us to go ahead and do everything we could. Mister Bennet ought to be here by five-thirty"

Five-thirty!

That was almost two hours away.

"Can I stay with him?" she managed between sobs of her own now.

"I have to ask you to wait in the reception area, at least for the next ten minutes. I'm really sorry but we need to make him as comfortable as possible and slow down his vitals." Miranda was able to stand shakily. She gave Nigel a long loving look, and then knowing she must, tore herself away and opened the door back out of the little room. She felt as if she'd left her heart behind her.

Back in reception, she hugged Dan tightly. "Oh god Dan, I'm so so sorry, I'm so so sorry" she kept repeating.

It was too much. Miranda could feel her stomach churning. "I think I'm going to be sick" she managed and headed straight to the little customer toilet. Everybody in the building could hear what followed.

When at last she'd finished retching, she wiped her mouth with tissues, sipped a few splashes of water, and then sat herself down on the toilet lid.

"Please come back. Please come back. Please come back." She prayed fervently. What could she do? How could she have been so stupid?

"Please come back. Please come back. Please come back."

Freya knew that this was one of the crucial times for Miranda, and everyone else for that matter. Intervention was allowed.

"Unblock him" she whispered in Mirandas ear.

It took several attempts before Miranda's psychic senses picked up the thread.

The idea came like a blinding flash of inspiration.

She did her best to compose herself and closed her eyes as tightly as she could.

There was the big red button, floating in mind-space in front of her. She mentally added the two extra letters. It took a few seconds to coalesce and then there it was.

UNBLOCK

Miranda reached out with her mind and pushed.

Freya and Bee smiled at one another. "I think you both did rather well" Bee complimented her friend.

"Thanks Bee. I just checked the life plan again. Nigel is going to be fine."

"Ah good. I think I love Kevin as much as I like Dan Rapier." Then Bee added "Poor chap, he's really going through it. He wasn't this bad when his sister passed."

"Yes, I remember. Then again, they never really got on that well in the first place did they?" Freya remembered it well. Even though she had her own charge, she'd always liked Dan.

"Naa. All this 'blood is thicker than water twaddle is complete bollocks. Anyway, shall we go and get Kevin? That was crafty what you did there. Who did you leave him with anyway?"

Bee smiled with a twinkle only her very best friends would have recognised. Freya gasped "Norman? You're telling me you're getting it on with Norman?" Freya laughed. "Oh Boudica, I've known you almost two thousand years and you're still full of surprises"

The two friends laughed as they melded back into the multidimensional ether stream.

The first thing Andrew noticed was the change in background noise. He had been pacing around Sedgewood trying to make sense of this peculiar, eerie, version of the little town. He was also doing his utmost to avoid the other inhabitants.

They all wanted to know what was going on, where he'd come from, and whether anybody was looking for them. Quite a few people wanted to know if their homes and belongings were still intact.

Kristen had tried to attach herself to him and had offered him every carnal pleasure which existed. Andrew had declined the offer reasoning that even in the most desperate of times he wouldn't have gone anywhere near her.

The Hammer and Tong boys had invited him to come and get plastered with them as they played pool and table football.

When Andrew had dressed as Trevor Cooper, it had been a joke. These two had made it a lifestyle.

Andrew had again declined the offer.

Martin the troubadour had offered to play a few of his songs for him.

There was no chance Andrew was going to subject himself to four hours of woe-is-me songs, even if they were set to a reggae beat.

There were plenty of other offers too.

Andrew had taken to rising early, and going for long walks around the greenways which criss-crossed the little town in a bid to avoid as many interactions as possible. These people were, quite frankly, dreadful.

By Andrews reckoning, it was Friday afternoon. He was walking along the side of the canal. In the distance, he could hear traffic. The noises came all at once. He'd been walking along in silence, then he'd had a momentary dizzy spell, as if the earth had jolted around him, and then quite unexpectedly, yes, that was definitely a motorbike. He could hear cars in the distance too. Overhead, a low rumble drew his attention upwards to where the vapour-trail of a west bound airline painted the clear blue sky with a bright white smudge.

He stopped abruptly. 'Please let it be, please?' He offered up a silent prayer to whoever might happen to be listening. Was it possible? Could it really be? And then his phone beeped.

During his week in New Sedgewood, Andrew had continued to carry his little flip-phone with him and had faithfully charged it each night.

As he frantically tried to drag it from his pocket, a group of four young schoolboys came running towards him. Behind them, complete with dogs and prams, were the boy's mums. Andrew was dumbfounded.

He *must* be back.

In the place he'd been, there were no children.

The trio of mums all looked at him curiously as they approached, with one of them saying "It's Mister Morton isn't it? The vet?"

Andrew was speechless and in the same moment,

overcome with a visceral rush of relief.

His phone beeped again. As the boys and mums disappeared further down the canal path, he managed to fish his phone out and open it.

'Emergency, RTA, Spaniel.' The message said.

Andrew thrust his phone back into his pocket and began to run.

He was a fit man. He'd looked after himself and so he covered the three quarters of a mile to the surgery with ease.

The shock that greeted his arrival to the surgery was as great as his own relief at being back in what he thought of as the real world.

Miranda, now back in the reception area waiting anxiously, had burst into tears.

Everyone had questions.

Andrew, professional and dedicated as always, simply raised a hand and said "I had an emergency beep. Which room is the patient in?"

"Number four" a bewildered voice had answered, and leaving the reception staff and all the waiting clients in a state of utter astonishment, Andrew had gone straight in.

Three hours later, the door for the little theatre opened again, and Andrew and the pair of veterinary nurses who had been tending to Nigel came out.

Andrew looked at the sea of anxious faces and said quietly "He's going to be okay"

Miranda began weeping again, but this time the tears were happy tears.

Much had happened in the three hours. The news of Andrew Morton's sighting on the canal path had gone around Facebook quicker than an electric shock. The surgery staff had been texting their friends too, confidentially of course.

The news had reached the police station and the operations centre before Andrew had even finished his pre-op scrub. Police, television news crews and curious members of the public had swarmed to the little surgery from miles around.

Thus far, the surgery staff had managed to keep almost all of them outside in the carpark. Almost all, but not quite. There were three powerful looking men in dark suits waiting for Andrew to emerge from the surgery's little operating theatre. Obviously, they worked for some agency or other, but they weren't saying. One of them stepped forward and tried to steer Andrew by grabbing his Elbow. He hissed in a low voice "Mr Morton. You need to come with us"

Andrew turned to the man and said sharply "Get your bloody hand off me."

He conferred for a moment with the nurse who had spoken to Miranda earlier, and then stepped forward to speak directly to Miranda himself.

"Hello again." He said kindly "You must have been so worried. He's going to be okay you know? He'll be a bit bruised but as long as he gets enough rest and cuddles, he's going to be absolutely fine."
Miranda almost lept at him and proceeded to hug him so hard, he thought his ribs were going to break.
"Thank you, oh thank you so much."
"Please sir, we need to get you away from here now."
The dark suited man was more insistent now.
Andrew reasoned he was going to have to face the inevitable at some time anyway so it might as well be now.
"Very well." He answered huffily "Where are we going? I need to let my colleagues know when I'm going to be back on duty." He gestured the reception desk.
"We'll be quite certain to keep them updated on your behalf sir. Now, will you come with us please?" The man indicated a passageway which led to the rear of the building, there was a blur of movement, and then Andrew and the three dark suited men were gone.

"Can I see him now?" Miranda asked as the furore by the front doors began to erupt again. Evidently Andrew had been spotted by the press corps.
Just as she was being shown through, Sam, who'd been forced to wait outside, was finally able to slip past the doors.
He hugged Miranda first, and then turned to his lifelong friend.
"I just don't know what to say mate, you must be

devastated" he opened his arms and the two men embraced. "I am mate. I don't think I'll ever be the same again" Dan, usually so strong and resilient was almost sobbing again. "How did you know?"

"Barry the taxi came and found me" Sam answered, "There are some really wonderful people in this town"

"I know," said Dan between sobs, "and they really make up for all the horrible little scroats"

Andrew was invited to climb into a large black van. It took him completely by surprise when he was hooded and handcuffed. Who were these people anyway?

He had only been in the van for a few minutes when it stopped again. He was gently guided out of the van and taken across some tarmac and into a building. He knew he was at the school that the investigation team had commandeered. From beneath the hood, he could see the lines which were painted on the playground.

"Is all this cloak and dagger business really necessary?" he asked in a slightly weary tone.

One of the men answered "Well, not really, but the fing is, we enjoy it, see?"

Andrew didn't see, but he knew the type. He sighed heavily to himself. It was going to be another very long night.

Saturday morning in the Boycott house was unusually quiet. The evening before, having heard all about the terrible accident, Sargeant Robbin Gittings had called Dan and told him to take a few days off. "Don't worry about the special leave boy, I'll make sure you're covered." The sergeant understood only too well what a devastating blow the loss of such a beautiful and devoted friend would be.

Sam and Miranda had offered Dan the use of their spare room. They understood too that going home without Kevin was going to be heartbreaking.

"Where is he now?" Dan had asked as the three friends had squeezed past the relentless crowd at the little vets.

Sam had answered softly. "Barry the taxi said he'd take him to his brother until you decide what you want to happen for him"

Barry's brother was the local undertaker.

"I'm just too raw at the moment Sam, can you speak to him for me?"

"Yes of course mate. There's no need to rush anything is there."

The three friends had stayed up until the small hours again, and they'd emptied five more bottles before they turned in for the night. Unlike the last time, no one had wanted to eat, and mostly, they'd sat in front of the fire in a quiet, reflective silence.

Miranda had been awake again at 4am. Unknown to Sam, she'd quietly let herself out of the house, and walked through the neon lit darkness, back to the vets practice.

Emily, the nurse who was on duty that evening, had let Miranda in. She'd sat with Nigel until her phone had beeped at a little before six o'clock. It was Sam. He'd guessed correctly where she was, but he felt he ought to check anyway. He wanted to go and visit Nigel himself, so they decided to swap places so that at least one of them would be home when Dan woke up. They needn't have worried. Dan had gone to bed in the spare room, but he'd barely slept a wink himself. He'd heard Miranda go out, and he too knew exactly where she'd gone. He wouldn't have done a single thing any differently himself. He swallowed his tears. This was going to be harder than he'd ever imagined.

Andrew Morton gave a full and honest account of everything he'd encountered. Initially, he'd been questioned in what he could only assume was the headmasters office. Once it became apparent that he was going to talk freely, he was allowed to come out to the main school hall and address the entire team.

With cameras running, he began his tale from the point he'd last left the practice office.

Noone had wanted to miss this, it was packed.

The questions went on all night.

At last, in the insipid grey light of a wet December morning, Andrew Morton was driven home.

A heavy police cordon was placed around his house.

In his kitchen, the unidentified woman who appeared to be in charge of the investigation, had told Andrew "You're not under arrest. We don't believe that you're guilty of anything or that you've kept anything from us. However, we are going to have to ask you a lot more questions. Now then, you won't attempt to leave Sedgewood without telling us?"

"Are you kidding?" Andrew had been flabbergasted "I only just got back, and anyway, I have patients you know?"

The woman had produced a sheaf of papers.

"I need you to sign these non-disclosure agreements."

In the absence of a name, Andrew had decided to mentally refer to her as Madam X. He'd had enough of everyone now. He'd been practically mobbed in the other place, and now he was home, he was being treated like a criminal.

"Okay, I'll do it when I get up if you don't mind?" he answered huffily. "I'm shattered. I've had a hellish week, I need sleep, and I'm on rota again from Monday. Oh and do you lot plan on staying in my house, or can I have a little privacy now?"

"That's fine by me" Madam X had replied.

As long as Andrew kept his mouth shut, that was fine. She still didn't know what was going on, but the report she would send to her superiors later would suggest that inter-dimensional aliens were responsible. She dealt with that kind of thing a lot, only normally, the people only disappeared one at a time.

"She clicked her fingers at the three men in dark suits who had accompanied her, and then to his profound relief, once they'd all gone, Andrew was finally able to revel in the fact that somehow, unlike everyone else he'd met in New Sedgewood, he'd been able to come home.

In New Sedgewood, it took a few days before anyone realised that Andrew Morton had gone.

Martin the troubadour had been the first. He'd mistaken Andrew's graciousness for friendship. There was also the fact that to his mind, he'd been the first person to explain a little about where Andrew had found himself, and so Andrew owed him. He didn't know what, but he obviously owed him something. It was a trait he'd learned from Kristen who made it her life's mission to exploit absolutely any situation and everyone around her.

Kristen was angry when she heard about Andrew on the New Sedgewood grapevine. How could he possibly have gone? Yes, it was fair to say he'd rejected her at first, but he was bound to come around. How could anyone possibly resist her? Kristen wasn't used to people saying no. She decided to go out and seek comfort by robbing jewellery from locations all over the little town.

It was midweek when she got around to exploring Honey Lane. She knew that Renfield lived there now.

How had she ever become involved with that stumpy little twerp, she mused as she examined the houses to see if any had real insides, or whether they were just the external walls like so many of the other buildings.

True, he'd offered her guitar lessons, and he was quite good at fixing things in the kitchen and bathroom. Shame he hadn't been quite so adept when it came to fixing her own plumbing, but that was a price she was willing to pay if it gave her a crack at Pop Idol.

Kristen had started to call him Renfield too now, although she couldn't fathom why. Like all her fellow inmates, she was beginning to pick up on thoughtforms and consensus opinions which permeated both worlds. It was just there in her head.

She'd have been staggered to learn that without even realising, Toya and Renfield had begun referring to Kristen as Nosferatu.

As Kristen approached The Old Beehive Inn, she could see Toya's monster truck parked outside.

What on earth was she doing there? Surely those two couldn't have paired up could they?

How dare they! The treacherous cow! As for Renfield, the little shit. He was supposed to be heartbroken, and so he should be. She was the prize and he'd lost. He was supposed to be in there suffering from a broken heart.

She could hear laughter now as she got even closer.

The bastards!

Kristen stamped through the gate and began heading for the door. She was going to give them both a piece of her mind.

The guides looked on and sniggered.

"Well this could be dangerous" Martins guide, Tom Petty quipped.

"Yeah I know" answered his counterpart, Kristens own guide, Genghis Khan. "She hasn't got that much of a min to be giving bits away, no matter how small they are, bless her."

As the first few days after the accident and Andrews miraculous reappearance passed, Miranda and Sam took turns sitting with Nigel.

Dan came too for some of the shifts. Nothing could heal his heart from his terrible loss, but to sit with his best friends, and of course, Kevins best friend, gave him something to focus on.

True to his word, Andrew had turned up for work exactly as the rota had had him scheduled. He had to battle through a hoard of braying reporters every time he left his home and again when he arrived at the practice. They bombarded him relentlessly with questions.

"No comment." was the only answer they succeeded in eliciting.

In between sessions at the surgery, he made regular visits to the operations centre, voluntarily this time.

This had been a huge disappointment to the three goons who took their work very seriously.

He spent hours answering questions and putting pins in maps of Sedgewood. It wasn't long before it was apparent to everyone on the investigation team, that even with Andrews well-honed powers of observation and recall, there just wasn't anything else to tell.

How he'd managed to traverse dimensions was still a mystery. String theory had been discussed at great length, but nobody understood how it worked.

In the meantime, Elaine had messaged Miranda several times. Firstly to offer her support, and then to subtly ask

whether Miranda needed to have another confidential chat. So far, and it was Wednesday now, there just hadn't been a suitable opportunity. 'Can you come over tonight at about six-thirty?' Miranda had sent a text asking.
Sam had said that he'd stay with Nigel this evening.

Nigel had been moved into the special pen for post-op patients now. He was still drowsy from the painkillers he was being given, and he hobbled whenever he tried to stand. He was awake though, and he'd done his best to smile at his humans. He'd even tried to wag his tail, but the swelling had made it painful and he'd whimpered.
"He'll get there." Andrew had assured the anxious dog-parents.
Miranda kept having to stifle her questions. She desperately wanted to know where Andrew had gone when she'd blocked him. She'd have a chat with Elaine, and then perhaps she could find a way to talk to Andrew, well away from inquisitive ears.

The Wednesday morning surgery had finished, and Andrew squeezed into the front seat of his little mini. He'd had to kick up a fuss to have his little ancient runaround returned to him. The investigation team had impounded the vehicle and taken it away to one of their underground facilities somewhere when he'd first vanished.

The car had belong to his mum. Andrew had learned to drive in it. To him, it was far more than just a car.

He'd taken for granted that by now, somewhere on the chassis, there would be a tracker. He'd spotted the goons following him too.

Andrew was also sufficiently savvy to realise that the investigation team had probably planted tiny monitoring devices all over his home, and even in his clothing.

It wouldn't reward the team with any dividends, he'd already been thoroughly transparent.

Part of the reason was so that Andrew could be grabbed at a moment's notice if he even thought about breaching the gagging orders he'd signed.

Had they bugged the surgery too? he pondered as he pulled out of the little car park, narrowly avoiding squashing an over-enthusiastic reporter. Of course they had. If he'd heard his own tale, and he'd been on the investigation team, he would have done exactly the same.

Andrew was still trying to make sense of his strange experience. He'd searched the internet and had found websites which were devoted to the concept of timeslips and people who had experienced alternative realities. A surprising number of the accounts had come from rational, plausible witnesses. Andrew found that part reassuring. One thing that continued to puzzle him though, was why hadn't he met anybody nice?

Everybody he'd encountered had been dysfunctional and quite frankly, more than a little dislikable. That lot from the church for instance. What a horrible group of people. No wonder they'd all grouped together. Birds of a feather and all that.

Prior to his extraordinary experience, Andrew had already read numerous character assassinations in the newspapers. Nothing had prepared him for the reality though. He shuddered as he drove down Elm Tree Road. As someone who did his best to remain non-judgemental and open minded, he never wanted to meet any of that lot ever again. Not even if they rematerialized back in the real Sedgewood. A terrible thought occurred to him. What if he suddenly found himself back in the other place, trapped with all those…Andrew mentally filtered out all the uncomplimentary words his brain was offering and put in, people.

His musing continued as he drove slowly home.
Those dreadful people. That strange syrupy woman for example, she'd actually offered herself to him.
Then there was that songwriter bloke. His tea was good, but he had as much personality as the average paving slab.
Then there had been that peculiar man dressed entirely in camouflage. He was the one who liked sneaking into

people's houses Andrew remembered.

Andrew quickly checked his mirrors. The goons had temporarily vanished. He pulled over to the kerb and put the car in neutral.

He still had his phone.

The one thing he'd omitted from his statement was the bit where Roger Parkinson had been running for his life. Andrew had completely forgotten.

He had photos, and he knew exactly who the dog was, he'd operated on the same springer spaniel on the Friday of his return.

By some miracle, the investigation team had overlooked his phone.

Of course, he thought. They'd only searched him *after* he'd come out of the operating room and whisked him off to the school.

He chuckled as he thought about his trip to the headmasters office.

He'd been in full PPE. He'd left his phone in the little tray by the scrubbing up sink, and that was where it had stayed until he'd retrieved it on his brief visit back to the surgery to check on Nigel's wellbeing, that Saturday morning.

Andrew decided not to take any chances. If the photos were still on his phone, it opened an entirely new set of questions. Rather than take it out here, he needed to find somewhere private.

What was it that grubby little songwriter had said?
He could hear the singers voice saying
"Oh yeah? Probably. Roger's been here longer than any of
us. I don't think that springer likes him. He said at one of
the meetings that it's the Boycotts dog, but they're not
here"
And then, "It's really weird you know. Everyone's cats and
dogs are here, but not the people. I've got no idea how it
works, but they just seem to look after themselves."

Andrew immediately thought of Miranda and that nice
husband of hers, Sam. Given the circumstances, despite all
the cloak and dagger nonsense, Andrew needed somebody
not connected with the investigation to talk to. Someone
sane. Someone who, unlike the goons, wouldn't hurt a fly.

He indicated to pull out again, worried that he might have
been observed. Everything looked normal he reassured
himself, and even if there had been a micro camera
somewhere in the car watching him, he just looked as if he
were contemplating things. Given the circumstances, who
wouldn't?
Nigel would probably be well enough to go home on
Friday morning. Perhaps he could slip a discrete note to
Miranda when she came to collect him?

Andrew didn't know yet, but the goons had been called away to another job.

The commanding officer who'd received the report from Madam X was closing the investigation. It was probably just another inter-dimensional leakage, exactly as she'd suggested. The files in the deep underground store held hundreds of examples already.

Apart from the vet, nobody else among the missing appeared to be a great loss to society. There was no doubt in his mind that the personal files on all of them had demonstrated that repeatedly.

In twelve months' time, they would be declared missing, presumed dead, and then the government could seize all their assets. Nice little earner that one, although it didn't cover a fraction of the cost of the investigation.

Madam X had been reassigned. On the same day, the vet had reappeared, Max Bancroft, in front of almost thirty livestream cameras, had vanished from the House of Commons. Nobody had the slightest clue how he'd done it or where he'd gone.

In Blocked World London, Max Bancroft was currently curled up on the floor of the spar shop, just down the road from Downing Street.

He'd walked the deserted central London Streets for three days.

He'd had to sleep in his little office at Westminster. Without security personnel to let him in, he was excluded from most of the buildings he usually frequented. Even the special place where the ladies would administer 'punishment' were closed to him.

Strangest of all were the silent underground stations. Oddly, the escalators were still running. In the absence of people, the rats didn't need to hide anymore. Bancroft had fled back up from the depths of Victoria underground station as if the spectre of Dennis Skinner himself had been in pursuit.

Eventually he'd found himself walking past a car dealership in Pimlico. It was owned by one of his brothers from the lodge. He'd been in here before.

To his delight, he'd been able to get into one of the offices and gain access to the keys of the supercars which were lined up in the glittering showroom. He picked out the key for a bright red Porche and attempted to drive it straight out through the huge plate-glass window, just like they did in the films.

It hadn't occurred to him that the glass would be toughened. Luckily for Bancroft, he hadn't been able to build up enough speed to hurt himself.

He abandoned the Porsche and found a spare set of keys for a Range Rover which was parked in one of the spaces on the forecourt.

For several hours, he'd driven around the streets of Belgravia and Kensington. In Chelsea, he'd realised that for the first time ever, the streets were free of litter. The air was cleaner than he'd ever known it too. He didn't like it.

He drove out through Hammersmith and Chiswick and

followed the A4 until it became the much broader motorway, all the while, his mood kept flitting between anger at his situation, and a desperate desire for his nanny.

He kept heading west until he reached the Reading turn off. He was nearly there. Nanny, who had looked after him until his forty third birthday, had a house in Caversham. He still visited her even though he was almost forty-five now. Whether she was there or not, Nanny would have the medicine he needed. Nanny, like everyone else, was gone. The house was unchanged though, and it didn't take him long to find what he was looking for.

In a safe place behind the kitchen dresser, had been the fat bag of Columbian dancing powder she'd been holding onto for him. In the cellar, where the padded manacles still dangled from their hook by the door, he found an Aldi grocery bag crammed with sweet smelling home-grown.

After that, he hadn't known what to do, but Downing Street had seemed to call to him with an irresistible tugging. Perhaps if he stopped off at the secret armoury at Windsor on his way back, he could blast his way in? He still had his automatic coded access pass for the emergency operation centre in his wallet. Thank the great Maggie-god-rest-her-infernal-soul, that he hadn't left that behind.

He fantasised as he drove. At last he would be able to sit behind the big desk in number ten.

The trip to the armoury was fruitful. Bancroft remembered how to use the equipment from his army cadet days at Eton. Soon, all of Downing Street would be his, but first he needed a drink and some cigarette papers.

Consequently, now here he was, curled up in a corner of the unattended Spar shop, binging on Frosty Jacks and Jazz-cabbage roll ups. For the first time ever, he'd managed to roll one of his own. Nanny would have been so proud of him.

Elaine had hugged her friend and presented the inevitable carrier bag. "I thought I'd just go straight for a box" she said as Miranda had peered inside.

"I'll get you a glass" Miranda had answered "but I'm going to be sticking with tea this evening. I've had enough alcohol to float a small liner over the last few weeks." She went on to explain "I just realised a couple of nights ago when I was sitting with Nigel. It was almost six o'clock and I really wanted a drink. It's become far too much of a habit."

Elaine commiserated. "I know what you mean, it's just too easy isn't it?"

It was true, ever since Roger Parkinson and Taxi Keith had gone, Miranda had been self-medicating.

"I think it was guilt driven" she continued explaining as they sat down in front of the wood burner.

Elaine had given the disappearances a lot of thought too since the dramatic events she'd witnessed on the House of Commons live feed.

"What did happen exactly? With Andrew Morton I mean?" Miranda explained all about the big red UNBLOCK button and finished by saying. "Honestly Elaine, I feel so guilty, do you think I should bring them all back now?"

"I understand what you're saying Miranda, but I still can't help thinking that with the exception of Mister Vet, what you did , well, it was a good thing wasn't it? Especially with all the stuff that's come to light about those wappy church people. Getting rid of Bancroft was brilliant!"

Miranda allowed herself a half smile. "I hear what you're saying, but I have to know where they go."

And that was the crux of the matter.

Just where did the people she blocked end up?

The two friends discussed the possibilities for the next hour, and then Elaine said "Would you do it again? You know, now you know you can bring people back? Just imagine how much good you could do in the world?"

"It's tempting, but the only way I can ever decide that, is by talking to Andrew and finding out where he went. Besides, since he came back, I haven't tried it with anybody else. To be honest Elaine, I don't think I could cope with any of the others if they did show up again."

Sam had arrived home a little after midnight. "He's sleeping peacefully now" he'd reassured Miranda who'd come downstairs in her dressing gown. "Sorry love were you asleep?"

"I think I had too much caffeine" Miranda admitted. "You go on up, I'll be there in a little while."

From the comfortable sofa in front of the wood burner, Miranda listened to Sam settling down for the night. Another reason she'd been drinking so much wine was that she just couldn't sleep a lot of the time. She scolded herself again. This has to stop!

She pulled her special National Trust blanket from the back of the sofa and allowed her thoughts to wander.

The wood burner was barely alive when she woke up again. Upstairs, Sam was still asleep. He worked from dawn until dusk virtually every day during the summer. December and January were the exact opposite, in winter, he took every opportunity to sleep.

Miranda was surprised to learn that it was almost 7am. She reached out for the remote and flicked on the television. Miranda wasn't a great fan of breakfast television. She'd appeared on it herself several times as the result of articles she'd written. As she flicked through the channels, she came across her two least favourite presenters. To the nation, they played the role of boy and girl next door. In the studio, Miranda knew from personal experience, they were egotistical diva on steroids, and obnoxious super-controlling brat.

Miranda had to know.

As the pair on screen wittered away, Miranda closed her

eyes and pushed the big red button one more time.

The wittering stopped immediately. The guests who had been sitting on one of the sofas looked dumbly at the vacant sofa where the two presenters had been sitting just moments before.

Miranda glanced at the little clock on the mantlepiece. She allowed the little second hand two complete rotations, and then she closed her eyes again.

UNBLOCK

On the screen before her was chaos. The two bewildered, and now silent presenters had reappeared.

Miranda turned the TV off again, satisfied.

Well, that answered that then. Apparently she really could bring people back if she wanted to.

Miranda had another question. She'd discussed it the night before with Elaine. When was she going to tell Sam?

Most of the time, Miranda and Sam came at things from the same perspective. Most, but not always. Sometimes Sam would get very angry with the injustices of the world and sometimes, he would show a compassionate side and highlight a thought that perhaps Miranda hadn't considered.

Miranda in turn, was gracious and accepting of some people, and irritable and impatient with others. Woe betide anybody who'd actually manage to upset Miranda to the point where she'd made them a project.

While Nigel was recovering, and while Dan Rapier was grieving; the secret would have to remain with just Miranda and Elaine.

The remainder of Thursday had gone by uneventfully until, "How are we going to juggle this in the morning?" Sam had asked as he'd bustled around the kitchen that evening. "I'm going to need the van for the market, unless I go later of course."

Miranda was relieved. She'd been trying to work out how to get a moment with Andrew where she could ask him about his experience.

Picking her words carefully. She answered "I know you want to be there Sam, but honestly darling, I'll be fine. I reckon our lovely boy will be pretty dopey anyway."

"Oh I realise that, but how are you going to get him home?" Sam thought for a minute and then said, "I'd have asked Dan, but I know he's going back to work today."

"I've been thinking about that too." Indeed, Miranda had thought about little else for hours. Freya whispered an idea into Mirandas psychic ear. "I thought I'd ask Barry the Taxi. I want to be able to thank him properly for everything he's done anyway." Phew, that might well be the perfect solution. Nigel would get a lift home, Miranda could talk to Barry to thank him, and most importantly of all, she'd have a good opportunity to talk to Andrew Morton, although she still hadn't worked out how she was going to ask him about what had happened to him during his weeklong absence.

Miranda wanted to change the subject now. "Has Dan said anything to you about Kevin yet?"

"Oh hell! I meant to tell you." Sam looked dismayed.

"Oh?"

"Well I had a message from Brian earlier."

"Yes?" Miranda asked wondering what had happened now

"Well, he said he'd put Kevin into a special Dog coffin in the, you know, the cold store?"

"Yeah…?"

"Well he went to check on him this morning, and the box was empty. Kevins gone."

"What!" Miranda was horrified "Oh my god Sam, what are we going to tell Dan?"

"I have absolutely no idea" Sam had answered "Brian said he just couldn't think of any rational explanation. The box was there, but Kevin wasn't in it. Oh, and he said that he had only just gone to tidy Kevin up, but there wasn't a trace that he'd ever been in the box."

"Oh Sam, that's…I just don't know what to say"

"Me neither." Sam had answered.

Standing listening by the kitchen door were Freya and Dave Allen. They smiled at one another. The spirit guides knew exactly what had happened.

The surgery had seemed unusually quiet when Mirandas taxi had pulled up outside. The investigation team who'd been based at the school, had attempted to leave quietly under the cover of darkness. A pack of journalists had followed them. The few newshounds who had remained for that last day, had reluctantly had to acknowledge that they just weren't going to get anything out of Andrew Morton. When the news had arrived the previous morning, that two television presenters had vanished and then reappeared on live television, they'd gone too.

The more curious Sedgewood residents had suddenly decided en-masse, that their pets needed a check-up. The other three partners had divided the workload among themselves, recognising that their still slightly beleaguered colleague already had quite enough on his plate without being interrogated by an inquisitive stream of hamster and terrapin owners. By Friday, there were only the staff and the owner of a usually very talkative parrot, who had apparently lost his voice.

Miranda had been able to go straight into the recovery suit where Nigel was waiting expectantly. Andrew was waiting patiently too. Andrew had smiled warmly at Miranda. "Jus you? I was half hoping Sam would be here again. He's an absolute gem when it comes to gardening knowledge isn't he?"

Apparently Andrew and Sam had been having long conversations about growing things while Sam had been visiting Nigel.

"He had to go to the market this morning, he's there ever

Friday." Miranda had been about to say 'Andrew, I'd really love to have a chat with you,' when she realised that Andrew had put his finger to his lips and was now trying to pass her a small piece of paper.

Miranda, not knowing what else to do, took it.

"I don't know whose listening in" the piece of paper said. Andrew immediately passed her another. He'd evidently prepared a longer message on a series of post-it notes.

"Spooks" said the next message, and then a third saying "I think they've bugged everywhere"

This wasn't at all what Miranda had been expecting. She barely had time to react before he'd passed her a forth note.

This one was longer.

"They made me sign a gagging order, but I'd really like to talk to you" Miranda looked at him and he indicated she should turn the paper over.

"It's about where I went. I saw Nigel"

Miranda felt her knees go weak but managed to remain composed.

A fifth piece of paper was thrust toward her.

"Can you meet me at Sams allotment? 2pm today?"

Miranda nodded her head affirmatively.

Andrew held out one last piece of paper, "Just carry on as if we never had this conversation" and then he held his hand out, indicating she should return the little stack of post-it notes to him. He crumpled them and then deposited them in the contaminated sharps container.

The rest of the visit was fairly routine, although to anyone who'd been genuinely listening, the dialogue between

Miranda and Andrew was strangely stilted. It was as if they were rehearsing a play for the first time and they hadn't learnt their lines yet.

"Here's his prescription. He'll need to come back on Monday for a thorough check. Don't overdo it and just let him do things at his own pace for a few days."

Miranda had thanked him and having signed a pile of paperwork at the reception desk, had slowly led the still hobbling, but very happy Nigel, outside to the waiting taxi. She was relieved to get home. Unlike Taxi Keith, Barry the taxi was a lovely man, and she normally had all the time in the world for him.

The joy of having her beloved Nigel back was a little tainted though. Miranda had been completely unprepared for the conversation which had just taken place. She hadn't imagined for a second that Andrew would willingly volunteer anything.

She'd seen snippets of him saying 'No comment' on the news. If that lot couldn't squeeze him, how on earth was she going to be able to get him to talk. By some unseen miracle, that wasn't an issue anymore.

Miranda certainly didn't feel unsafe in meeting him at Sams allotment. Given the time that she and Elaine had put into research, she didn't doubt his integrity at all anymore.

At this time of year the plot would be deserted. She wondered why she hadn't thought of that herself. Sams little tea shed would be perfect.

At 2pm, when Andrew appeared at the allotment, Miranda was surprised to see him fully kitted out in running gear. The fluorescent trainers especially betrayed the fact that they'd never been worn before.

"I gather that the investigation team has gone now, but I couldn't take any chance that they might have bugged my clothing" he explained.

He'd been able to change, he said, in the gents at the Wizards Staff. Afterwards, he'd temporarily left the rest of his clothes with Molly at the sportswear stall on Sedgewood's market. He'd go back and collect it all later. Miranda had already unlocked the shed and the little gas heater had taken the chill out of Sams special space.

Miranda indicated an armchair. "Have a look at this?" Andrew had handed her his little phone. There on the screen was a beautiful photo of the unmistakeable figure of a frantic Roger Parkinson, with Nigel in hot pursuit.

"Oh my god!" Miranda had gasped. "Can you tell me all about it?"

Over the next two hours, Andrew manage to tell Miranda what had happened in as much detail as he'd told the investigation team.

Miranda, for her part, managed to get through the entire conversation without betraying herself once.

When Andrew was finished he said at last "So what do you think about all that then?"

"I really don't know what to say." She'd replied honestly.

"That was definitely Nigel" the vet had stated earnestly. Miranda couldn't help laughing at that point.

"Oh bless him, he always did love chasing that horrible Roger. I don't get it though. How could Nigel have been here, and at the same time, wherever it was you were?"

Andrew took a deep breath and said "Miranda, I've been

looking at loads of YouTube about alternative realities, have you ever heard about a phenomena called Quantum Superposition?"

"I have as it happens" Miranda had always loved science fiction and she'd been a regular subscriber to the New Scientist too.

They chatted for a few more minutes and then Andrew had climbed to his feet saying. "I really appreciate you listening Miranda, I really needed someone to talk to. I know you're bound to tell Sam, but if you could keep it to yourselves, that would be great?"

"Oh heavens, yes of course"

"I'd better go and get my kit, the market will be packing up now. Oh. By the way, I hadn't had a chance to look, but if you've accepted my friend request, I'll send you the photos of Nigel?"

"Brilliant Andrew and thank you. I can't tell you how much your trust in us means."

Later, when Sam came home, he was so preoccupied with Nigel that they didn't manage to get dinner until after 9pm. They ordered a curry to celebrate. Sam thought that Miranda's elevated mood was simply down to Nigel's return. He still had no idea at all of the burden Miranda had been carrying ever since the day before their wedding anniversary when Miranda had blocked first Roger and then Keith.

They both went to bed feeling a lot happier that night and while Sam went to sleep almost immediately, Miranda lay awake planning. Some things just couldn't be changed, but there was still something really important she had to do.

Nothing much grew during the winter months, but Sam still had a few jobs to do at the allotment. There were swedes and parsnips to lift, sprouts to be cut and compost to be spread. Sam had taken a greatly healed Nigel with him.

Miranda had checked to make sure all the doors were locked and then she settled herself onto the sofa.
Once again, she sat back and imagined the big red button, only this time, she was going to block herself.
She remembered something Andrew had said, so she opened her eyes and flicked on the television. Then she went and fetched her laptop, which she opened the screen and then clicked on the live feed for the webcam for Trafalgar Square.
She settled herself and focussed again.
BLOCKED
The television had gone silent. Beside her, the laptop screen was fuzzy and said NO SIGNAL.
The television showed only snow on the screen.
For an instant, Miranda was terrified. An icy grip took hold of her chest. She'd have begun hyperventilating, but just then Nigel came into the room and nudged her with his nose. Oh no, she groaned inwardly, was Sam back?
A quick look out of the front window told her that Sams familiar little van wasn't parked where he usually was.
Miranda was fascinated and terrified at the same time. Was she really in that other place? If she was, would she be able to get back?
She had to resist the urge to follow Nigel through to the kitchen.

UNBLOCK

The television seemed to come to life again, and so did the laptop.

Miranda giggled to herself. "I did it, I really, really did it"

The timing was perfect. With Christmas approaching, Miranda had a break from work until January now. Sam would be busy making up stew packs and taking orders for Christmas vegetables from all his regular customers.

Miranda went and got a coat from the hooks by the front door. If what Andrew had said was accurate, the weather in the Blocked World version of Sedgewood would be just as cold as it was here. Miranda was going to go and have a look at the other Sedgewood.

She made herself comfortable on the sofa again and blocked herself.

Just to be absolutely certain, she unblocked and blocked herself again twice more.

Satisfied now that she could easily replicate the transfer, Miranda set out to explore.

Blocked World was fascinating. Miranda had taken on board everything she'd learnt from Dan Rapier about the real Sedgewood's surveillance cameras. She was also mindful of the lesson she'd learned from Andrew Morton. It was vital that nobody here saw her. She'd still have been able to get away she reasoned, but she just didn't want the hassle of having to interact with anyone.

She was delighted to realise that just as Andrew had said,

Nigel's protective presence was reassuring. Miranda was glad that he was there too.

Quantum super position, well fancy that! she'd said to the happy spaniel as they set out to indulge in a little careful exploration of what this amazing, if a little peculiar place, had to offer.

With Nigel by her side, being careful to duck out of sight whenever she thought she heard anyone, Miranda began the short walk into town.

There was music belting out of the windows at the Wizards Staff. On the pavement outside, the unmistakeable figure of Taxi Keith was having an argument with the Hammer and Tong boys.

"She's my bloody girlfriend…."she'd heard one of the voices shouting.

Realising the raised voices would soon attract other attention, she decided to head off up to the Forty and investigate a few of the shops and houses.

Nigel spotted Roger before Miranda did. Before Miranda could stop him, the delighted spaniel had sprung into action and hurled himself at the creepy stalkerish fantasist. There was nothing Miranda could do about it.

She would have to come back another time. Perhaps later or perhaps in the early hours of tomorrow morning? She was about to unblock herself when the thought struck her, what if she rematerialised in the middle of town and somebody saw her there?

Miranda hurried home to the New Sedgewood version of the privacy of her own house.

Back at home in the kitchen, she tuned her mind into the big red button.

UNBLOCK

When Miranda appeared right in front of him out of thin air, Sam, who'd just been making himself a cup of tea, almost fainted.

Miranda allowed him to compose himself and said

"Oh Sam, I've got so much to tell you. I couldn't tell you before, I almost didn't believe it myself. I think we'd better sit down."

Sam had managed to sit quietly listening while Miranda had told him the whole story, including her confession to Elaine, and her subsequent confidential meeting with Andrew.

Sam, for his part, was calm, and completely intrigued. He reach down to rub Nigel's head.

They sat in silence for a few minutes while the enormity of Mirandas confession sunk in.

At last he spoke.

"So almost everything's the same?" and then to Miranda's immense relief . "Oh well done on sending the beastly bunch away! And Roger for that matter, well all of them actually."

He chuckled to himself and then lapsed into quiet contemplation again.

When he did speak, his question caught Miranda totally unprepared. "You know if you go…let's call it over there…?"

"I have to Sam, I need to know that nobody's actually genuinely been hurt. If they're just living out their lives, that's fine, I can live with that."

"Well when you do go" Sam smiled now "Can I come with you?"

"Oh my! Oh Sam. I'm so sorry, I hadn't given it a thought. I've only just found out that I can go and come back myself."

Miranda paused for thought for a few more seconds and said "I don't see why we can't both go. When were you thinking of?"

"Well I'll be far too excited to sleep tonight. Look, it'll be dark soon. Presumably, it'll be dark over there too, and just like here, they'll all be settling down for the night? How about we pop over for a couple of hours after dinner?" And so that was what happened.

They'd both dressed in warm, dark clothing. First Miranda Blocked Sam, and then just a few seconds later, she sent herself to join him in their alternative living room. Back at home, Nigel had been asleep in his bed in front of the wood burner. No doubt he'd be on the sofa before they returned.

In their home in Blocked World, Nigel had obviously come home after his fun chase with Roger and was sitting comfortably on the sofa now. Neither Sam nor Miranda could work out how Nigel had been able to get through the closed doors.

That had been Dave and Freyas doing. In New Sedgewood, all the guides had taken full responsibility for the wellbeing of all the pets.

The New Sedgewood version of the Boycott house was chilly, but New Sedgewood Nigel didn't appear to have noticed. In fact New Sedgewood Nigel was as perky and active as his counterpart in the source world had been prior to the accident.

Together this time, Miranda and Sam had gone out to explore.

Nigel had wanted to come with them, but fearful their beloved friend might give them away, they'd decided to leave him at 'home.'

They were walking past Joys little shop when Sam had an idea. "How about this" he whispered to Miranda in the darkness. "If everything grows here the same way it grows at home, what if you could pick a crop here, and then take it back to our Sedgewood?"

Miranda thought about this for a moment and said, "What exactly are you thinking about Sam?"

""Well you know I've been working on our mushroom plantation?"

"Yes, go on."

"Truffles" he said brightly. Miranda had to laugh. Dear Sam, just plain earthy and practical.

"I think that's a brilliant idea" she whispered back, and then "Oh my word, what on earth is that dreadful racket?" They carefully worked their way down Honey Lane until they could peer through the hedge. In the conservatory of The Old Beehive, Renfield and Toya were practising their own unique version of Silent Night. "I think that's the most appalling thing I've ever heard, come on, lets carry on"

"I don't think I'll ever be the same again" Miranda laughed and they set off again on their quest to explore a little more.

They spent another hour tip-toing around. The music from the pub had stopped now, but the lights were still on. There didn't appear to be anybody on the streets at all. That was hardly a surprise though, under a sky of almost unbelievable clarity, they could feel the impending frost. "I'm freezing" Miranda had vocalised what they were both thinking.

"Me too, shall we go home?"

"Yeah, I think I might be able to sleep now. We can come back tomorrow."

They made good progress now they'd abandoned creeping around, and soon they were back in the New Sedgewood version of their treasured little house.

"Are you ready?" Miranda had asked.

"Almost. I do wonder though" clearly Sam was pondering another question.

"Go on Sam?"

"Well, you know if we already own something?"

Miranda began to pick up on Sams idea, "Yes, carry on?"

"Then taking it with us isn't stealing is it?"

"No, I suppose not."

Sam grinned broadly. "I've got a secret savings pot in the bedroom"

Miranda's eyes widened. "Oh Sam, you beauty. Actually, so have I."

"No?"

"Erm, yes!"

They laughed and took turns to indicate the stairs.

"After you"

"Oh no madam. After you."

Back in the kitchen with their respective bundles, Miranda turned to Sam and said, "Right then, anything else before we go?"

Sam disappeared into the lounge and came back clutching a bottle of whiskey.

He opened the fridge, it was, as usual, loaded with cheese.
Oh Miranda, do you think it replenishes, like the way Andrew described about all the shops?"

"I don't know love, but that would be pretty wonderful if it did. I could just block myself and come over here with a shopping bag. Grab me a piece of truffle cheddar while you're there will you? We can check tomorrow and find out whether we've discovered an everlasting cheese stash."
Sam grinned broadly.
"Ready now?" she asked one last time. Sam nodded, and Miranda unblocked him.

Back in his own proper kitchen, the temperature was noticeably warmer.
Sam had opened the fridge and taken out an identical piece of truffle cheddar. That had been a great idea. Sam could always manage a piece of cheese. Truffle cheddar was an expensive luxury. Now they had a block each.
A few seconds later, Miranda too reappeared. Much to Sam's surprise, she was carrying Nigel.
"I just couldn't leave him behind" she gasped, out of breath now "Have you been feeding him sausages again?"
Sam grinned cheekily "Okay, I confess, just one or two."
Miranda put Nigel carefully on the floor. He went straight to his biscuit dish.
There was a thud and a patter of paws as the other Nigel jumped down off the sofa in the lounge and then came through to investigate. He glanced up at Miranda and then at Sam, and then he too went to investigate the biscuit dish
For just an instant, the two Nigels stood side by side, but didn't appear to notice one another.
The air around them seemed to shimmer briefly, and the two springers merged into a single form.

Untroubled by what had just happened, the single Nigel looked up at his humans and gave them his best 'I'm hungry' face.

Sam glanced over at the table. Happily, the two blocks of cheese were still a pair.

Miranda and Sam looked at Nigel and then at each other.

"We have to go back" they said to one another at exactly the same time.

It was almost midnight when Dan Rapier opened his front door.

"Oh!" he said "Miranda, Sam, is everything okay?"

He tried to take everything in in a snapshot.

Miranda and Sam had brought Nigel with them.

And then Dan realised he wasn't looking at Nigel.

There in front of him was the most wonderful sight Dan had ever seen. With his familiar beaming spaniel smile, and a happily wagging tail, stood Kevin.

The night before Christmas Eve, in the comfortable warmth of Sam and Miranda's lounge, Dan Rapier and Elaine were chatting while Sam was busy preparing a small feast in the kitchen.

Miranda had said she was nipping out to the shops and so they expected her to return imminently.

Kevin and Nigel were happily chasing one another around the garden.

"I see you managed to give Tom the slip then?" Dan was smiling.

"Indeed I did" Elaine had answered "It's his works do tonight. Just as well seeing as we're having our first proper coven meeting"

Dan laughed, "I hadn't thought of it like that, but yes, I suppose you're right. Are we actually allowed to discuss, you know, the secret?"

By now both Dan and Elaine were fully up to date with Mirandas Superpower and all that had happened so far.

"I think that's why we're here this evening" Elaine had answered. "I'm so glad you're back with Kevin now. Miranda told me yesterday what had happened. How did you explain his reappearance?"

Dan sighed. "That was really awkward. I hate being untruthful. Luckily, Brian had confidentially told the sarge that Kevin had vanished. I just played dumb and said that I'd heard a noise at the door late in the evening last weekend, and when I looked out, there he was. It's a miracle!" Dan smiled again. The truth was his version of events was actually true if you omitted Sam and especially Mirandas involvement.

"Being that there's no other explanation, we've just planted the seeds that it was a deep concussion, and that he'd come around again all on his own. Of course, I have had to keep him away from everybody for a couple of days. His recovery might seem to be just a little bit too miraculous."

"Oh Dan, I'm so pleased for you, both of you."

Sam came through the door, armed with a huge platter laden with cheese and other delights. At the same time, the front door clicked and Miranda could be heard along with the familiar clunking of bottles.

When she did come in to join the other three, they were all equally surprised to discover that Miranda was clutching a grocery basket which contained four bottles of Dom Perignon.

"Blimey Miranda, that lot must have cost an absolute fortune." Was Elaines reaction.

Miranda smiled and said "Oh I didn't pay for them. I've been over to the, you know, the other side. You know Tim always keeps a couple in the special fridge in the Wizards?"

"Oh Lummy," it was Dan's turn now "I thought he only kept a maximum of two bottles at a time?"

Miranda grinned.

"He does, I had to go yesterday too. I left the first two out under the fuchsia in the front garden so they'd be cold enough." Sam laughed approvingly.

"I thought The Wizards was where young Hammer and Tong were hanging out?"

"Oh they've fallen out" Miranda replied knowingly.

"Kristens been shagging both of them and they've only just found out."

"Brilliant!" said Sam.

"And by the sound of it, she'd been having a fling with Taxi Keith too. Urrrghh." Miranda did a mock shudder. "Anyway, Sam, do the honours will you?" She handed Sam one of the bottles.

Elaine chipped in "How on earth did you find out all that lot already? How much time have you been spending visiting?"

Miranda looked over at Sam and then back to her friends "Oh, we've been over for at least a couple of hours every morning and evening since we found Kevin."

Dan was impressed. "And nobody's spotted you yet?"

It was Sam's turn now. "We think that Roger Parkinson knows as he's been hanging around the end of our road a lot. He's pretty easy to spot though, and depending on where we set off from, he's easy to avoid anyway."

"Didn't you say he'd been pally with Taxi Keith?" Dan asked.

It was Mirandas turn now. "He was, but Keith's gone back to his mums in a huff. It was Roger, we think, who told him all about Tim, James, and Kristen."

"But how on earth do you know all this?" Elaine was impressed.

"Oh that's easy, shall I open another?" Sam picked up a second bottle of the fine champagne and continued. "It's a dreadful noise to listen to, but there's so little else going on, that Renfield writes a song about just about everything. I'm surprised he doesn't try singing about his latest trip to the bathroom."

The conversation flowed freely as Miranda and Sam revealed some of the other things they'd learnt over the course of their visits. Both Dan and Elaine were eager to ask something though.

"You know when you go again next time?" Dan asked for them both.

"Yes?"

"Can we come with you? I think we'd both love to see for ourselves?"

"I think that's a great idea" Sam answered. "We'd been wondering whether you'd consider it anyway."

Miranda took a turn to explain a little more. "Sam's going to be really busy as Spring approaches, so it's not going to be practical for him to keep coming. We thought it would be a lot safer if one or both of you came with me sometimes?"

"Especially on the shopping trips" Sam laughed and then said. "After all, you're our most trusted friends, and we'd love for you to get some benefit from this" he paused momentarily.

"Superpower" Miranda finished the sentence for him.

"Fantastic!"

"Yeah, that's fabulous, oh thanks you two."

The conversation carried on as the four friends discussed where in New Sedgewood they would like to go.

"Free dog food forever" Sam had said to Dan.

"And free, well, free all sorts really" Miranda had said to Elaine.

After a while Elaine decided it was time to vocalise her other main train of thought.

"Miranda, you know when you blocked Max Bancroft. Where do you think he went?"

Miranda had been considering this too.

"You know I said I'd sent those Brekkie Brats away as an experiment? I've been reading the transcript from the interview they did about it afterwards.

They said that they'd been in a place which was identical, but without any people. What I'm guessing is, Max Bancroft ended up in another version of Westminster."

"Oh that's beautiful" Dan was laughing now.

"Right then" Elaine was fishing in her jeans pocket "What do you think about blocking a few other tossers?"

Miranda didn't have time to answer before Dan said "Actually, I've been thinking about that too. I ran the plate of the hit and run driver who clobbered Nigel. I've got his name here"

Dan too began fishing deep in his trouser pocket and said "Actually, I know it's a bit rude, and I really don't expect you to do this Miranda, but I made a list?"

"So did I" Elaines voice added.

"And so did I" it was Sams turn now.

"Oh! Oh! Ahhhh, Um, Erm, Oh dammit! So did I" Miranda confessed and then threw her head back to laugh.

"Can you imagine it?" Elaine asked, "A world full of tossers where the only company they have are others exactly like them?"

"That's such a wonderful idea" Sam was definitely in favour.

"I can live with it" Dan added his voice of approval.

"Oh my, well now, just think of all the good we can do? Right then, I'm up for it. Politicians, creeps, criminals, perverts. Let's do it!"

Miranda rubbed her hands together as if warming them and then with a twinkle in her eye said

" Okay then. Who shall we send away first?"

The Arrival of Regit.
Jeremy Moorhouse

Regit hadn't planned to come to Earth and certainly not to Chippenham, but now he's here for a few days, he might as well find out a bit more about these peculiar Bipeds and their strange habits and customs.

Phillip and Kelly and their neighbour Lucy are left with dozens of questions when Regit arrives in their midst. Why does he keep dressing like different pop stars from the 1980's? Where does he go when he disappears? Does he really eat cat biscuits? Who redecorated the bathroom?

Moley saw Regit arrive. He has some questions too. Major Thompson of the 'Special unit' also has questions.

Crop circles, Adam Ant, Big cat sightings in the countryside It's all going on.

Follow Regit as he tries to make sense of our crazy world.

"An absorbing flight of imagination based on a sound philosophy of how good life could be.

A fun-filled lark underpinned by environmental awareness and a knowledge of the old English landscape and the mystical secrets of the country's ancient sites. A very enjoyable read with some laugh-out-loud moments. Good Stuff.

Emmetyville.
Jeremy Moorhouse

You've never seen a holiday destination quite like this before. See the visitors and locals of a small Cornish town with microscopic precision. So who really controls what goes on? Learn about the secret workings of the 'Special club' . Find out who the town underwear thief is and discover his dark past. Follow the local WPC Veryan Bolitho and her Sargent, Lowenna as they try to bring order out of the chaos. You'll meet a host of charming characters as you follow them through their weekend shenanigans. You'll laugh until it hurts and when you finish reading, you'll definitely want to visit.

Emmetyville 2.
Jeremy Moorhouse

In a beautiful Cornish fishing town, a lot goes on behind closed doors. Donald and Sylvia want to retire here, so do their friends Norman and Marjorie. The men want to grow cannabis plants, their wives, at 73 and 74 years old, have a nice little pension enhancer in their sex toys business. Meanwhile, Cowboy and Uncle Keith want to be real drug smugglers. Hotel manager Paul just wants to make it through the day. Rachael and Jimmy are deeply in lust. Sargent Lowenna and WPC Veryan want to know what the hell's going on, and who keeps stealing Lowenna's knickers? Denzel Sprygelly is due out of prison any day soon, and if there's going to be pie, then Denzel want's a slice! Laugh until it hurts. You'll be glad you picked this one.

The Twelve Groans of Christmas.
Jeremy Moorhouse

Christmas had it coming!

We all know somebody who doesn't enjoy the festive season, right?

Well, this book is for that person.

You'll recognise the characters, you might even wince as you remember when that particular thing happened to you.

What you'll most certainly do, is laugh.

"I laughed so much at this I bought copies of it for everyone at work. Jeremy Moorhouse, you make me howl!"

Jeremy Moorhouse.

You can find out more about Jeremy Moorhouse on his Facebook page, Author and Storyteller, Jeremy Moorhouse.

If this offering has made you laugh, please leave a review on Amazon or the Facebook page. Thank you.

Printed in Great Britain
by Amazon

40159997R00169